"Oh, Mallory, you shouldn't have let me in," Michael said huskily.

Unsure of his meaning, Mallory looked into his eyes, and couldn't breathe.

"Nobody looks this sensational at six o'clock in the morning! I love your hair when it's all tousled and wild like that. And whoever said flannel nightgowns aren't sexy hasn't seen you in this one. Gorgeous." He slid his hands around her waist. "Really beautiful," he murmured, lowering his head slowly toward her.

His mouth captured hers, his lips warm and seeking. The kiss was gentle, yet demanding, and Mallory responded instantly to his closeness. The soft fabric of her nightgown seemed thin as gossamer as he pressed against her, the smooth, cold leather of his jacket igniting a heat inside her that nothing could cool. Mallory felt an uncontrollable urge to run her hands over Michael's body, to drive away the chill and kindle a raging fire there . . . a fire that would consume them both. . . .

WHAT ARE *LOVESWEPT* ROMANCES?

They are stories of true romance and touching emotion. We believe those two very important ingredients are constants in our highly sensual and very believable stories in the *LOVESWEPT* line. Our goal is to give you, the reader, stories of consistently high quality that may sometimes make you laugh, sometimes make you cry, but are always fresh and creative and contain many delightful surprises within their pages.

Most romance fans read an enormous number of books. Those they truly love, they keep. Others may be traded with friends and soon forgotten. We hope that each *LOVESWEPT* romance will be a treasure—a "keeper." We will always try to publish

LOVE STORIES YOU'LL NEVER FORGET
BY AUTHORS YOU'LL ALWAYS REMEMBER

The Editors

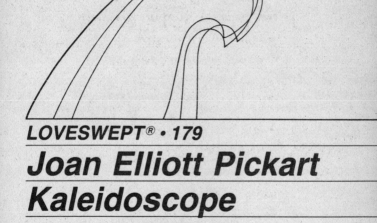

LOVESWEPT® • 179

Joan Elliott Pickart
Kaleidoscope

BANTAM BOOKS
TORONTO • NEW YORK • LONDON • SYDNEY • AUCKLAND

KALEIDOSCOPE
A Bantam Book / February 1987

If you would be interested in receiving protective vinyl
covers for your Loveswept books, please write to this address
for information:

Loveswept
Bantam Books
P.O. Box 985
Hicksville, NY 11802

ISBN 0-553-21801-8

Published simultaneously in the United States and Canada

PRINTED IN THE UNITED STATES OF AMERICA

O   0 9 8 7 6 5 4 3 2 1

For Sally Smith, who puts
me on the right plane, at
the right time, and gets me
where I'm supposed to go.

Thanks for the cookies, Sal.

One

The telephone rang shrilly in the dark room, and a slender hand reached out and solidly whacked the alarm clock. The telephone rang again.

"Phone," a voice mumbled. "Phone? Oh, the phone!"

Mallory Carson sat up in bed and fumbled for the telephone with óne hand and the switch on the bedside lamp with the other. Accomplishing both feats, she blinked against the sudden light.

"Yes. Hello," she said into the receiver.

"Mallory? Hello, dear, this is your mother."

"Mother?" Mallory said, now fully awake.

"Yes, your mother. Everyone has one at some point in their life, you know. How are you, dear?"

Mallory rubbed her blue eyes and glanced at the clock on the nightstand. "Mom, it's one o'clock in the morning! Why are you calling? Is something wrong?"

"Wrong? No, not exactly. I just need a small favor."

"At one o'clock in the morning?"

"Don't shout, Mallory. It's not ladylike. I was wondering if you would mind coming downtown and picking me up?"

"Picking you up," Mallory said, nodding slowly. "Downtown. At one o'clock in the morning."

"You're beginning to sound like a parrot, repeating everything I say. It's a very simple request. My car is unavailable at the moment, and I need a ride. I'll explain everything when I see you. Will you come?"

"Yes, of course," Mallory said, squeezing the bridge of her nose and closing her eyes. "Where are you?"

"Across the street from the Community Center."

Mallory's eyes shot open again. "Across from the— The police station is across from the Community Center!"

"Bingo! I'm in the slammer. See you soon, dear. Ta-ta."

"Mom? Mother?" Mallory said to the dial tone. She slammed the receiver into place, threw back the blankets on the bed, and ran toward the bathroom, stripping off her nightgown as she went. "I'll wring her neck," she muttered. "I'm too old for this. She's driving me crazy!"

The February Tucson night was damp and chilly as Mallory drove above the speed limit to the police station. She'd grabbed the first clothes she'd put her hands on—a faded pair of jeans, a red sweatshirt that boasted KIDS ARE PEOPLE TOO, and tennis shoes that had definitely seen better days.

The attempt to bring order to her long, black hair had brought little results, and the thick, wavy hair was in wild disarray. Her lips were pursed tightly together and her fingers were drumming on the steering wheel.

"Jail!" she muttered as she speeded up to beat a red light. "My mother is in jail. Other mothers knit and bake chocolate-chip cookies, but Clarissa Carson? No-o-o, not Clarissa Carson. She's in the clink at one o'clock in the morning."

As Mallory approached the police station she reduced her speed, deciding this was not the time to get a ticket. She pulled into the parking lot and immediately slammed on her brakes as a sleek black sports car roared into the lot from the opposite end and whipped into the parking space Mallory had been heading for.

Well, thanks a bunch, she thought. She pulled in next to the sports car, shut off the ignition, and pushed open her door, hitting the black car with a solid thud.

"Hey! Watch it," a deep voice yelled. "That's an expensive car you're beating up on."

Mallory slammed the door of her compact with more force than was necessary as a tall man strode around the end of the sports car toward her. The amber lights illuminating the parking lot cast an eerie glow, transforming the man into a large orange-tinted creature.

"I didn't hurt your car," she said, tilting her head back to look up at his orange face. He was over six feet tall, she decided, considering the pain she was getting in her neck from her vantage point of five feet five. He had extremely broad shoulders and was dressed in a T-shirt and jeans, which were probably blue, but in this light appeared a rather sick shade of green. Between his orange hair and the shadows flickering across his orange face, he was definitely giving her the creeps. "Excuse me," she said stiffly, "but would you please get out of my way? I really need to go inside the station."

The man hunkered down beside his car and ran his hand over the door. "In a minute," he said gruffly. "Yeah, okay, you didn't dent it or chip the paint. You really should be more careful."

"Me?" Mallory said, planting her hands on her hips. "You were the one driving like a lunatic! You cut me off when you zoomed in here. Oh, forget it," she said, inching around him. "I have more important things to do than stand here and watch you fuss over your shiny toy."

She slung the strap of her purse over her shoulder and started off at a brisk pace, only to be passed a moment later by the man, whose long legs carried him rapidly across the parking lot and into the building.

"He's really into zooming," she muttered. "That was a very rude, orange person."

Mallory pulled open the door and entered the brightly lit building. A uniformed officer sat behind a high desk, a few other officers were milling around, but beyond that it was quiet. Very quiet. The man from the parking lot was speaking in a low voice to the officer behind the desk. Both he and the officer looked up as she approached.

"Excuse me," she said, "I'd like to—"

"Wait your turn," the tall man growled. "I have urgent business here."

"Well, so do I!" she said.

The man shifted to face her, and one thought crossed Mallory's mind: This man definitely was not orange!

He was various shades of thick, blondish hair, and golden tan on a face that was unbelievably handsome. He was a pale green T-shirt stretching across a broad chest and binding muscled biceps; he was snug blue jeans molded to slim hips. He was great big brown eyes. He was in Technicolor! And he was gorgeous.

"Look," the man said, frowning as he raked a large hand through his tousled hair. "I didn't mean to snap at you. I'm a little shook up at the moment."

Oh, the poor man, Mallory thought dreamily, her gaze riveted to his face. "I understand perfectly," she said, smiling sweetly. "You go right ahead and talk to this nice officer, and I'll stand here and wait my turn. No problem at all." Other than the fact that her mother was in jail. Sweet heaven, her mother was in jail! "But hurry up!"

The man eyed Mallory warily, then redirected his attention to the rather bored officer behind the desk.

"As I was saying," the man said, "I've come to collect Mary Louise Patterson. I'm Michael Patterson, her son."

Mallory's eyes widened. "You're Mikey?" she asked.

Michael Patterson's jaw tightened and he turned once more to Mallory, his eyes narrowing. "The name," he said through clenched teeth, "is Michael."

"Oh," she said, nodding, "of course. Whatever strikes your fancy. It's just that Mary Louise calls you Mikey."

"I know it! I know it, but I don't like it. Who the hell are you?"

"Me? Oh, I'm Mallory Carson. I came to get my mother, Clarissa."

"Ah-ha," Michael said, pointing a long finger at her. Mallory jumped. "Clarissa Carson is a menace! She's turning my mother into a juvenile delinquent."

"I beg your pardon. My mother was a perfectly normal person until she met Mary Louise Patterson a month ago. Your mother has led mine astray. She led her to jail, that's where she led her."

"Folks," the officer said, "this is all very fascinating, but could you take it somewhere else? Oh, and take your mothers too. They're not under arrest, they just think they are. I'll have them brought up. They're in the back playing gin rummy with a couple of winos we hauled in."

"Oh, good lord," Mallory said.

"Just why are our mothers here in the first place?" Michael asked, still frowning.

"Well," the officer said, "they were at the rock concert across the street at the Community Center. There was a rule about not taking pictures, but your mothers whipped out their cameras. When the security officer tried to confiscate the cameras, they whopped him with their purses. That wasn't a great example for those kids over there, so we brought the old gals in."

"Oh, good Lord," Mallory said again.

"Damn," Michael said. "It's that book they're working on. That damn book that *your* mother dreamed up, Mallory Carson."

"Mine! It's your mother who claims to personally know an editor in New York, who will be absolutely thrilled with this great endeavor. Don't blame this on my mother, Mikey Patterson."

"It's Michael!"

"Here we go again," the officer said, picking up the telephone. He dialed two numbers, then waited. "Bud? Bring up Bonnie and Clyde, will ya? Thanks."

Mallory folded her arms over her breasts and tapped her foot impatiently, absently noticing that her big toe had popped through the top of her threadbare tennis shoes. She cocked her head to one side, admiring the shade of polish on her toe. Raspberry Rain was very pretty, she decided.

A rumbly chuckle caused Mallory to lift her head and gaze up at Michael Patterson. He was looking directly at her, smiling, and her heart did a flip-flop at the transformation that had come over his stern features. The smile caused tiny lines to crinkle by his eyes, and revealed white teeth that were obnoxiously perfect. It was a beautiful hundred-watt smile. And it irritated Mallory no end that it belonged to a man who had said such derogatory things about her mother.

"Do you have a problem?" she asked, frowning at him. "I hardly find this situation amusing."

"The situation, no," he said, still smiling to beat the band. "You, yes. You don't look much older than a teenager standing there with your toe poking through your shoe. It's a cute toe, by the way."

"You're too kind," she said, then sniffed indignantly. "Your approval of my big toe just makes my day. And I assure you I'm not a teenager."

His gaze swept over her in a lazy scrutiny. "Mallory," he said, "I'm definitely aware of that."

She opened her mouth to deliver a snappy reply, but for the life of her couldn't think of one thing to say. Michael Patterson was no longer smiling. He was looking at her as though he could see through her clothes, and a tingling sensation started in the pit of her stomach and danced throughout her. He wasn't gawking or being lewd, but simply looking, as if he truly appreciated what he was seeing.

Tit for tat, Mallory thought, mentally shrugging. Heaven knew she'd given him the once-over, and he'd passed with flying colors. Goodness, he was handsome. And that body. Perfectly proportioned, tanned. Mikey had a lot going for him.

"Here they are," the officer behind the desk said. "Flash and Dash of the crime world."

"Hello, hello," Clarissa sang out.

"Greetings, children," Mary Louise said.

"Mother?" Mallory and Michael said in unison, their eyes wide.

The two tiny older women were dressed in black sweaters that buttoned to below their knees, black stockings appliquéd with pink butterflies, and black shoes with spike heels. Their hair was sticking straight up, held in place by some invisible force, and was a strange shade of blue-green.

"I've never seen this woman before in my life,"

Mallory said. The officer laughed. Mallory glared at him.

"Okay, I'll bite," Michael said, a frown drawing his tawny eyebrows together. "What are you supposed to be?"

"Punk rockers," Clarissa said, "into the heavy metal sound. We wanted to fit in when we went to the concert. We were doing fine until that sassy young man tried to take our cameras. I told him we were taking pictures of the audience, not the performers, but he didn't give an inch, said rules were rules. So, here we are, smack-dab in the slammer. It's been a marvelous experience."

"Oh, yes," Mary Louise said. "Very invigorating. And as a bonus, you've met Mallory, Mikey."

"It's Michael," he said tersely. "Do you suppose we could end this nightmare and go home?"

"What happened to your car, Mother?" Mallory asked.

"Oh, they said it got locked up for the night behind the fence at the Community Center."

"I'll bring you down tomorrow to get it," Mary Louise said.

"No, you won't," Michael said. "You're grounded! You're not leaving your house."

"Oh, hush, silly boy," his mother said. "You're trying to treat me as though I were a naughty child."

"Because you're acting like one! This caps it, Mother. I've had it. In the past month you two have ridden on the back of motorcycles with bikers named Sneak and Snake—"

"Snake and Jake," Mary Louise said.

"Whatever! You've gone into sleazy bars, walked

in a picket line without knowing what you were picketing, went for a ride in a hot-air balloon, and Lord only knows what else. Enough is enough."

"It certainly is not," Mary Louise said. "We're gathering data, taking pictures depicting a cross-section of America for our book."

"I knew it," Michael said, scowling at Mallory. "I knew it was for that damn book. This is *your* mother's screwy idea."

"Oh, no, we're collaborating," Clarissa said. "We both get to have our names on the cover."

"I think," Mallory said, "we should all go home and view this fresh tomorrow."

"Great idea," the officer said.

"Why don't we go to an all-night café and have some breakfast?" Mary Louise suggested. "Then Mallory and Mikey can get better acquainted. Wouldn't that be nice?"

"No," Michael said.

Oh, darn, Mallory thought. "We're leaving. Right now," she said, taking her mother's arm. "What in the world is that junk in your hair? Never mind. I really don't want to know. Good night, officer. Thank you for your patience."

" 'Night, folks," he said. "Good luck."

"We'll need it," Mallory muttered under her breath.

Outside Clarissa and Mary Louise walked on ahead, teetering precariously on their spike heels as they chattered about their exciting, adventuresome evening.

"Mallory," Michael said, his voice low, "we've got to do something about those two."

"We?" she repeated, glancing up at him. Oh,

good grief, she thought, he was orange again. But she could remember every detail of how he'd looked in living, breathing Technicolor. "I was under the impression that you considered this disaster entirely my mother's fault."

He sighed. "No, my mother is equally to blame. But they have to be stopped. Their antics are becoming dangerous."

"They're sixty-five-year-old women, Michael, not children."

"Life goes full circle. They're going through a stage, and they need a guiding hand. Look, could we have lunch tomorrow and talk about this? Between the two of us surely we can come up with a plan of action to slow down the dynamic duo."

Lunches were nice, Mallory mused, but so were romantic, candlelight dinners in cozy restaurants with strolling violin players. Oh, well.

"Are you free for lunch?" Michael asked.

"Yes, that would be fine. Shall I meet you somewhere?"

"That would probably save time. I'll have to get back to my office. Is Marie Callender's on Wetmore at twelve-thirty okay?"

"Yes indeed."

Michael stopped and placed his hand on Mallory's shoulder. She looked up at him questioningly.

"I'm sorry I was so abrupt with you," he said.

"*Rude* was the word that came to my mind," she said, smiling at him. "But all is forgiven. This was not what you would call a run-of-the-mill evening."

He looked directly into her eyes. "No," he said, "definitely not."

Mallory's heart started its tapdance again. She firmly told herself to stop gazing into the fathomless depths of Michael Patterson's eyes, but she didn't move. She simply stood there, staring at him, wondering what it would be like to be pulled against that broad chest, kissed by those luscious lips, and—

"Lunch," Michael said, his voice strangely husky.

"Who? Oh! Yes, lunch. Tomorrow at twelve-thirty. Good night, Michael," she said, and spun around and marched to her car.

Clarissa was waiting beside it, in all her blue-green-haired glory. After both she and Mallory were settled, Mallory maneuvered the car out of the parking space, making certain that she didn't come remotely close to Michael's vehicle. Her mother waved exuberantly to Mary Louise, but Mallory stared straight ahead, concentrating on her driving. At the exit she admitted defeat, and peeked into the rearview mirror. Michael was standing there in all his orange magnificence, watching her, his hands shoved into the back pockets of his jeans. Mallory drew a steadying breath before continuing on her way.

"Isn't Michael a handsome young man?" Clarissa asked.

"I really didn't notice," Mallory said. "Mom, about what you did tonight . . ."

"That was the first time I'd seen Michael, but, of course, Mary Louise has told me so much about her Mikey."

"Mikey," Mallory said, smiling. "He apparently isn't overly fond of being called that. I heard Mary Louise refer to Mikey when you dropped by that time to see me. I must say, Michael Patterson is quite different from the image I had in my mind of a 'Mikey.' "

"Then you *did* notice how good-looking he is," Clarissa said. "You'd make a marvelous couple, dear."

"Oh, no, you don't. Don't you dare start your matchmaking routine again."

"I wouldn't dream of it," Clarissa said, slouching back in her seat. "You pitched such a fit when I arranged for you to meet the butcher's son, I was thoroughly embarrassed."

"He was fifty-six years old! And the mailman's son is five feet two. The gardener's darling little boy has been married four times. Shall I continue?"

"You've made your point. But you must admit, Mallory, Michael is a hunk of stuff who really fills out a pair of jeans."

"Mother!"

"Don't be such a fuddy-duddy."

"I'm not a fuddy-duddy. It's just rather jarring to hear you talk so . . . so graphically. Really fills out a pair of jeans? For Pete's sake."

"Well, he does."

That was no joke, Mallory thought. He did wonderful things for T-shirts too. So, okay, he was a hunk of stuff, but sixty-five-year-old mothers weren't supposed to say things like that.

"I worry about you, Mallory," Clarissa said, sighing deeply.

"Me? *I'm* not the one who landed in jail tonight. I was sound asleep in my bed."

"Alone. And therein lies the problem. You need

a man in that bed with you. A sexy, virile son of a gun."

"Give me strength," Mallory said, rolling her eyes heavenward.

"With the right man," Clarissa said, laughing merrily, "you'd need all the strength you could muster. Now, Michael Patterson looks like he could—"

"Mom, that's enough."

"Your biological time clock is running, Mallory. You must give serious thought to having a child before it's too late."

"That was my twenty-ninth birthday we celebrated last month. I hardly think of myself as being over the hill."

"Time flies . . ."

"When I'm having fun? Bailing my mother out of jail in the middle of the night is not fun."

"You're avoiding the issue. It's time you were married and had a baby. I wish I was liberated enough to encourage you to have a baby, married or not. I'll have to work on my attitude about that. Men are such nifty creatures, though, and I want you to have one of them too. I realize you date a steady stream of young men, and from what you've said they're all very successful professionals in various careers. But goodness, dear, you hustle them in and out of your life so fast, I can't keep up. Aren't you ready to make a commitment to one of them? I do so want a grandchild, Mallory. Would you deny your own mother her dying wish?"

"You are not dying!"

"Well, I'll croak someday. Would you have me

check out never having known the joy of being a granny? Shame on you."

Mallory simply shook her head in dismay as she turned onto the driveway that led to her mother's large house.

"March yourself into that house," Mallory said firmly, "and go to bed. I, for one, am exhausted. I'd only just gotten in from a date and fallen asleep when you called; I was at the symphony the night before, and Alison and I spent Saturday in Phoenix shopping. This little jaunt was not on my schedule, and I have to be up early. I certainly hope you can get that glop out of your hair. I'll talk to you tomorrow."

"All right, dear," Clarissa said, opening the door. "Thank you for the ride. Oh, and do give some thought to the fact that Michael Patterson is an extremely handsome man. Ta-ta."

"Ta-ta," Mallory said wearily.

Once Clarissa was safely inside the house, Mallory headed back across town to her apartment. Sleep, she thought. She needed sleep. All she wanted to do was go to bed. Alone? Well, of course, alone. Yes, she wanted to get married and have children someday, but it wasn't that simple. She had every intention of being totally in love with the man she chose to spend the rest of her life with, and she hadn't fallen in love with anyone yet.

What her mother had said was true, she mused. She did date a wide variety of men. Many were from the affluent social circle she had grown up in, and all were bright and successful. They enjoyed the good life and few were particularly interested in settling down. That was fine with Mallory, for while the men she dated were all nice, they were basically boring. Oh, a couple had hinted at being ready to marry and have a family, but she hadn't been enthralled with the men themselves.

Was she being too picky? she wondered. Did she expect Mr. Perfect to leap out from behind a bush and declare himself madly in love with her? Was she asking too much to want a man who was warm, intelligent, and caring; liked children and dogs; and was brave, courageous, and bold? A man who melted her right down to her socks with his mere touch and kiss? A handsome, virile son of a gun, who really filled out a pair of jeans? A man like Michael Patterson?

"What?" she said. "Where did he come from? Go away, Mikey!"

At last in her bedroom, Mallory pulled off her holey tennis shoes, flung herself across her bed fully clothed, and fell instantly asleep.

Two

Since Mallory had shut off the alarm when the phone had rung the previous night, she overslept. Muttering uncomplimentary things about her mother, she rushed through her shower. After coiling her thick black hair into a figure eight at the back of her head, she reached automatically for her jeans. Then she hesitated, remembering her luncheon date with Michael.

No, she told herself, it wasn't a date, it was a meeting to discuss their wayward mothers. But still . . .

A half hour later Mallory pulled open the door and entered the Honey Bee. The sound of children's laughter reached her ears, and she smiled. The Honey Bee was one of the finest day-care centers in Tucson, and it was hers, her dream come true.

*   *   *

At precisely twelve thirty Mallory stepped into the entryway of Marie Callender's, shifting her blazer carefully over her arm to hide the still damp area of her skirt where she'd sponged off the grape jelly. Mint-green wool dresses did not fare well under the onslaught of twenty busy children, she had discovered too late, but there was nothing she could do about it now.

She saw Michael Patterson before he noticed her, and she scrutinized him from head to toe, every magnificent inch. He was leaning casually against the bar, chatting with another man, and was dressed in a brown suit and tie with a pale yellow shirt.

Colors, she mused. Both last night and today she was acutely aware of the colors of Michael, from his multishaded blondish hair, to his bronzed tan, to his clothing. Maybe it was because he had been orange when she'd first seen him. How whimsical to think of a man in terms of colors. What color was strength? Gentleness? Laughter? Laughter was yellow, like sunshine. Strength was black; powerful, heavy, dense. Gentleness, a dusky blue. And Michael Patterson making love? Earth tones— rich, vibrant, basic.

"A kaleidoscope," she whispered, her gaze riveted on Michael.

As if sensing her presence, he turned his head and their eyes met across the room. He set his glass down on the bar and said something to the man beside him, although his gaze remained locked with Mallory's. He pushed himself away from the bar and began walking slowly toward her.

Mallory had the irrational urge to bolt out the door, to put as much distance as she could between herself and Michael Patterson. He approached her with the confident gait of a hunter stalking its prey, and she felt trapped, pinned in place. A shiver swept down her spine, and her heartbeat echoed in her ears.

She was acting ridiculously! she told herself. She was in a crowded restaurant, surrounded by people, meeting a man to discuss their naughty mothers. Her lack of sleep was causing her brain to short-circuit. But a hunter was green, to blend in with the jungle or forest where he would capture what he sought. . . .

"Hello, Mallory," Michael said, extending his hand.

"Michael," she said, hearing the unsteadiness in her voice. She lifted her slender hand and placed it in his large one, feeling the warmth travel up her arm and suffuse her body. Warmth, the color of honey.

"You look lovely," he said, still holding her hand. "Although there was something very enchanting about your appearance last night too."

"If you like ragamuffins," she said, slowly withdrawing her hand. "I was rather thrown together at the time."

"Your hair was marvelous, tousled and wild, like a gypsy."

"Oh, well, I prefer it more tidy," she said, touching the coil at the back of her head. "Don't you think we should get a table? I don't imagine you have much time."

"I made a reservation," he said. "The table is ready. Shall we go in?"

The restaurant was decorated with beveled-glass windows and a multitude of antiques, which lent it an Old World quality. Mallory ordered avocados stuffed with shrimp; Michael the ham sandwich. After the waitress had left them Michael leaned back in his chair, folded his arms across his chest, and frowned slightly. Mallory adjusted her napkin across her lap to cover the damp spot, then met his gaze.

"Is something wrong?" she asked.

"No, not really. I've been hearing the name Mallory Carson for the past month, since my mother met yours, but I realize I know very little about you. Except, of course, that you have a jailbird for a mother."

"We have that in common," she said, smiling.

"I think we should discover what else we have in common."

"Why?"

He appeared rather startled, then laughed. "Why? Because I want to know who you are, Mallory Carson, other than a very beautiful woman. What do you do to pay the rent?"

Beautiful? Mallory repeated silently. Attractive, maybe. Wholesome, pretty, but beautiful? Oh, rats. Michael Patterson wasn't one of those fast-line hustlers, was he? They were the color of mud.

"Uh-oh," he said, smiling at her. "You think I'm dishing out a bunch of bull by telling you you're beautiful, right?"

"I'm taking it under advisement," she said,

frowning slightly. "Beautiful is a bit much. Try attractive and I'll go with it."

He chuckled. "Nope," he said, leaning his arms on the table. "The beautiful stays. I'm an honest, upfront, tell-it-like-it-is guy. Now that we've established the fact that you're beautiful, what do you do for a living?"

"I own the Honey Bee."

"You own a bee? That makes honey? One bee?"

"No." She laughed. "It's a day-care center. I'm licensed to handle twenty children. I've got twenty already and have started a waiting list."

"Good for you. You like kids, I take it?"

"Adore them."

"But you don't have any of your own?"

"Not yet."

"Have you ever been married?"

"No. Have you?"

"No," he said, his jaw tightening. "And I don't intend to marry . . . ever."

The waitress arrived with their lunches, and Michael moved back to give the young woman room to set the plates on the table.

Mallory studied Michael's face for a long moment before directing her attention to her food. He certainly was uptight on the subject of marriage, she thought. Since he'd never been married, it wasn't because he'd been through a nasty divorce. Interesting. And rather disappointing in a vague way. Oh, that was silly. Why should she care if Michael Patterson was a hard-core bachelor? It certainly made no difference to her. He appeared to be about thirty-six or -seven, so was apparently quite adept at sidestepping serious commitment. More power to him if that was how he chose to live his life. It wasn't any of *her* business.

"What have you got against marriage?" she asked. Oh, good Lord, had she said that? Talk about having a big mouth.

"I simply don't feel it's a realistic way for people to live. Life is difficult enough with its daily stresses and pressures, without jamming two individuals under the same roof and telling them to exist compatibly no matter what the circumstances are. People need space, room, privacy."

"But what about companionship? Sharing? Loving?"

"It's out there when you need it."

"Perhaps. If you're equating loving with sex. I'm referring to love, being in love. You can't find that in a singles bar, enjoy it for a while, then go merrily on your way."

"I don't find my life lacking because I've never been in love," he said. "In fact, from what I've seen, love can be a depleting state of mind at times. I'm not saying there aren't good marriages, because there are. My parents were happily married for thirty years before my father died. But statistics have proved that too often marriages are a disaster. I spend many hours trying to glue some of those people back together."

She speared a shrimp. "What do you do for a living?"

"I'm a divorce lawyer."

"Oh, I see," she said slowly. "That explains things a bit. You don't exactly meet with the *crème de la crème* of marriages."

"Not hardly," he said, frowning. "It's almost inconceivable at times what people are capable of doing to the one they had professed to love. I'm talking about emotional abuse more often than physical."

"Why do you specialize in divorces?"

"I got a bachelor's degree in psychology before going to law school. I enjoy both fields, and I've been able to incorporate my psychology background into some of my divorce cases. My first responsibility is to try to reconcile the couple. If that fails, I make myself available should they need someone to talk to. Divorce is a traumatic experience for most people. I make it clear that I'm not a doctor of psychology, but many people are hesitant to seek the further help they need."

"I'm impressed," Mallory said. "I'm sure there are a great many attorneys who wouldn't take such an interest in their clients." She smiled. "And I'm kind of glad you're not a full-fledged doctor of psychology. I'd be nervous then, wondering if you'd end up knowing me better than I know myself."

"I'll settle for just getting to know you," he said, taking her hand in his.

There was that warmth again, Mallory thought, feeling the heat tingle up her arm. The honey-colored warmth of Michael Patterson's hand. It was nice, just very, very nice.

"Wait a minute," she said, jerking her hand free. "If you've studied psychology so thoroughly, surely you can figure out what's wrong with our nutzy mothers."

Michael threw his head back and roared with laughter. "Mallory," he said, grinning at her, "those dear old ladies aren't crazy. They're bored! They could also be voicing their displeasure over the fact that they don't have any grandchildren. My mother claims that all her friends have grandchildren, then she glares at me. I'm an only child, and Mother mentioned that you are too."

"Bored?" Mallory said. "So they get themselves thrown in jail? Go tooling off with bikers named Sneak and Freak?"

"I think they were Snake and Jake."

"Who cares? The point is, their behavior is a bit extreme to be merely expressing boredom, or the desire to bounce a baby on their knee. My mother has been a widow since I was ten, and hasn't worked a day in her life. She's never had problems with filling her time before."

"Nor has my mother," Michael said, and took a bite of his ham sandwich. "You know, there is always the possibility that they sincerely want to do this book of theirs. If that's the case, then we're not being entirely fair by not taking them seriously. No one is too old to have a dream."

"What a lovely thing to say."

"It sounds like the title of a song, but it's true."

"Try this one on for size," Mallory said, leaning across the table toward him. "The two little darlings are matchmaking and have concocted this elaborate plan to bring you and me together."

He frowned. "I never thought of that. My mother has tried that a time or two in the past."

"Oh, mine is the master of the game. She didn't lighten up until I threatened to move to Siberia and open a day-care center there. Michael, how are we to know what is really going on in their heads? We have quite a list of possibilities here. If the book is truly important to them, they should do it. Exhibiting a bit more common sense in the process, of course. But if this is boredom or a con, I would most cheerfully wring their motherly necks."

"I thoroughly agree. The tricky part is to figure out what they're up to."

"We could ask them?" Mallory said hopefully.

"Ha! Mary Louise Patterson will lie through her teeth if she feels she has a 'reasonably reasonable reason,' as she so astutely puts it."

"So would Clarissa Carson, I guess," Mallory said, sighing.

"Do you know that my mother faked having a sprained ankle once because she'd found a nurse she wanted to fix me up with? Mother declared she needed round-the-clock care, then kept dreaming up reasons why I should come to her house. I caught her though. I popped in unexpectedly, and she had gone bowling!"

Mallory laughed. "That was very innovative."

"Well, all we can do is wait and watch for now. Stay alert, Mallory. Try to pick up on any clues that might help us figure out what's going on. We'll keep in contact with each other and compare notes."

"Yes, of course," she said, and concentrated on her lunch. Strictly business, she mused. Michael was making *that* plain enough. One minute he was telling her she was beautiful, and the next minute she was nothing more than somebody's kid. How deflating. How depressing. How disappointing. Well, what did she want? she asked herself. Michael Patterson to toss her on top of the table and ravish her? Oh, how ridiculous.

"On to more interesting topics," he said, bringing her from her reverie. "Tell me about the Honey Bee."

"It's marvelous," she said, setting down her fork and smiling with excitement. "It's bright, cheerful, happy. We take two- to four-year-olds. I have three women working for me, and they're all wonderful with children. I majored in business administration at the U of A, and minored in child development. Admittedly I had the money from my father's estate to get the business started, but the hard work and the building of a solid reputation is all mine, earned by many, many long hours."

"Why a day-care center?"

"I love children. I always hated being an only child. I used to fantasize about having a houseful of brothers and sisters. Now I have twenty kids surrounding me all day."

"But they're not really yours. A parent shows up at a certain time and whisks them off. Then you're free to spend the evening as you choose."

"Meaning?" Mallory asked, frowning slightly.

"I don't know," he said, shrugging. "It's a nice setup, I guess. You can play at being a mother without any of the real responsibilities that go along with it."

She stiffened in her chair. "Putting on your psychologist's hat, Mr. Patterson?" she said tightly. "I don't care for your insinuation that I'm playing some kind of frustrated-mother role at the Honey Bee. Those children are important to me."

"Hey, I'm sorry," he said, covering her hand with his. "I really do apologize, Mallory. I was thinking out loud more than anything, picturing the Honey Bee in my mind. I never thought about day-care centers, because I've had no reason to. Working mothers are fortunate to have a place to leave their children, and be assured they'll have loving attention."

"But?" Mallory said, still frowning. "I have the impression you haven't finished."

"Well," he said slowly, "I'm realizing that we have a great deal in common. We're trained professionals, offering a much needed service. Yet we have the luxury of staying just on the edge, away from emotional involvement. I give maximum effort to talking, say, to the chronic wife-beater, but I don't walk in that man's shoes, nor take him home with me at night. We both deal in touching people's lives, Mallory, but at the end of the day we can put it all on a mental shelf, and not think about any of it again until the next morning."

Color Michael Patterson gray, Mallory thought suddenly. A confusing, complicated, foggy, gray. She wasn't sure she liked what he was saying in regard to her and the children at the Honey Bee. It sounded cold and clinical, devoid of emotion.

"You're still frowning," he said. "I take it you don't agree with what I've said?"

"I don't know. You're opening doors to areas I've never given any thought to. It's confusing, and rather disturbing."

"I'm just pointing out how much we have in common. It's very rare for me to find someone who operates on the same plane as I do. Rare, refreshing, and very special. I'm glad I've met you, Mallory Carson."

Mallory blinked once slowly, then realized that

at some point Michael had begun to stroke her hand with his thumb. The words *rare, refreshing, and special* echoed in her mind, as the now familiar tingling sensation began in the pit of her stomach and traveled throughout her. Michael's voice was the color of rich, smooth indigo velvet, and seemed to fall over her like a cloak. She felt nearly hypnotized by his deep brown eyes, and her pulse quickened.

Suddenly a strange sound erupted from beneath Michael's jacket and he quickly undid the buttons and reached inside.

"My beeper," he said. "I'll have to call my office. Will you excuse me for a moment?"

"Yes, certainly," she said.

She watched as he strode across the room, noticing the power, the authority in his muscular frame, in the way he carried himself. She drew a steadying breath, then scooped up another forkful of shrimp.

Michael Patterson was, she decided, without a doubt the most unsettling man she had ever met. When he gazed at her with those chocolate-brown eyes of his, she couldn't think clearly. That tingling that ran through her was different from anything she had experienced before.

She wasn't sure she liked the effect he had on her. And she wasn't sure she liked Michael himself. The things he had said about her lack of emotional involvement with the children at the Honey Bee weren't true—were they? Did she actually lock the door at six each night and not think of those kids again until the next morning?

But to say she was *playing* at being a mother,

with none of the ongoing responsibilities . . . The nerve of the man! That was rude. Orange and rude, just like he'd been in the parking lot of the police station.

The best plan of action regarding Mr. Patterson, she told herself, was to stick to the business of their harebrained mothers, and view him as Mary Louise's son and nothing more.

He slid back into his chair at that moment and smiled. "Ready for some homemade pie?" he asked.

"Yes, it's delicious here. I'll have coconut cream, please. Was there a serious problem at your office?"

"No, just a change in scheduling. I'm supposed to speak with an accused murderer, who's trying to get an insanity plea."

"A murderer?" Mallory said, her eyes widening.

He laughed. "It's interesting work; the human mind is fascinating. Can't you sense when one of the children at the Honey Bee is upset or disturbed about something?"

"Well, yes. There's a four-year-old named Amy who gets very nervous whenever she spends the weekend with her father and his new wife. I don't think she ever adjusted to her parents' divorce, and she can't understand why her father has a different family now."

"See? The slogan on your sweatshirt last night said KIDS ARE PEOPLE TOO. That's very, very true." He paused and looked at her, and she thought she would drown in his deep brown eyes. "Are you beginning to realize how much we have in common, Mallory?"

She forced herself not to be mesmerized by his beautiful voice. "I think we should concentrate on our mothers, Michael," she said. "And if they're matchmaking, we'll simply tell them we're incompatible."

"We are? Why?"

"Because I have no intention of becoming involved with a man named Michael. Everyone would point at us and say, 'There go the M and M's.'"

He laughed and shook his head. "That's great. The M and M's."

"It's a valid point. Besides, Mallory and Michael sounds like a vaudeville team. Or a matched set of poodles. Or—"

"Mallory," he interrupted, suddenly serious, "are you afraid of me for some reason?"

"Don't be silly," she said, straightening the napkin on her lap.

He tilted her chin up with one long finger, forcing her to meet his gaze.

"Do I frighten you?" he asked, his voice low. "That certainly wasn't my intention. Nor did I mean to insult you in any way about your work. You're a beautiful, intriguing woman, and I'm merely attempting to get to know you better. So far I like everything I've discovered about you."

Good! Mallory thought wildly. No! Wrong. She didn't want anything to do with this man. Of course, it might have been nice to experience just one tiny kiss from those sensuous lips of his, but she could live without it.

"Oh, Mallory," he murmured, dropping his hand to the table. "I really would like to kiss you. You have the most inviting, kissable lips I have ever seen."

Oh, dear heaven, Mallory thought. She wasn't

going to survive this. What happened to the nice, safe coconut cream pie? He wanted to kiss her? No kidding? Fancy that.

"Would you care for some pie?" the waitress asked.

"Yes," Mallory said, a trifle too loudly. "Coconut cream. And some coffee."

"I'll have pecan, please," Michael said, "and coffee too."

"Coming right up," the girl said, then hurried away.

"About our mothers," Mallory said quickly.

"I thought we covered that for now," he said, smiling at her. "I'd much rather discuss kissing you."

"Well, *I* wouldn't!"

"Why not?"

"Because it's not something people discuss. You just do it, for Pete's sake."

"I'll keep that in mind," he said, the smile growing bigger.

"Michael." She leaned forward. "If our mothers honestly have a dream about having a book published, they're in for a bitter disappointment. They have inexpensive cameras and don't know the first thing about photography. Those prints won't come close to looking professional. Besides, there are probably releases or something they have to get from people whose pictures they take. I don't want to see our mothers' dream shattered."

"But we don't know that it is their dream."

"I realize that. Oh, what a mess."

"We'll take it slow and easy for now; just be very

observant, see what clues we can pick up. What do you think? Shall we take it slow and easy?"

Mallory knew Michael Patterson was no longer talking about mothers. Her heart was doing the two-step again, and there was a weird feeling in the center of her stomach. Slow and easy? Ha! The man was a steam roller, a smooth talking, sexy hunk of stuff, who really filled out a pair of jeans. What? Where had that absurd thought come from?

"Here's your pie and coffee," the waitress said.

"Thank goodness," Mallory muttered.

Mallory concentrated on her pie as if it were the most fascinating thing she had ever seen. She ate it down to the last crumb, dabbed at her lips with her napkin, then slowly looked up at Michael. He was slouched back in his chair, his arms crossed over his broad chest. He was smiling one of his dazzlers, and Mallory frowned.

"Enjoy your pie?" he asked.

"Yes." Her glance fell on the untouched dessert in front of him. "What's wrong with *your* pie?"

"I don't like coconut cream. You just ate my pecan."

She plunked her elbow on the table and rested her forehead in her hand. "I don't believe this," she said, feeling the warmth of a blush creeping onto her cheeks.

"Hey," he said, jiggling her arm. "Do wonderful things for my ego and tell me I was the one who got you all shook up, not our wacko mothers. Puff up my male esteem, my fragile inner self, and say that I, Michael Patterson, blew your mind with my charisma and fabulous body. Come on, Mallory, make my day."

She lifted her head and burst into laughter. "I think you should make an appointment with the psychologist part of yourself and check out the stability of your brain." She paused. "I'm sorry I ate your pie."

He smiled at her, a warm smile, a comfortable smile. But then the amusement in his eyes slowly faded, replaced by a sexual awareness, by desire.

"Michael, don't," she said softly.

"Don't look at you, admire you, think about kissing and holding you? Why not? My reactions to you are honest. I won't pretend that I don't find you extremely attractive and desirable."

"And what's next?" she asked sharply. "We're both consenting adults, so why not jump into bed together? I don't indulge in casual sex, Michael. I usually don't take part in conversations like this either, but you leave me no choice. I really must be getting back to the Honey Bee."

"Mallory, I don't think for one minute that you have casual sex, or go bed-hopping all over Tucson. That wasn't what I was implying. I sense that you're an honest woman who doesn't play games in a relationship with a man. That's all I was doing: being honest. You *are* a very beautiful and desirable woman. Now, do you want to eat the coconut cream pie, or throw it at me?"

She smiled and shook her head. "Mr. Patterson, you should have gone into politics. You have a way of wiggling yourself out of situations with a very smooth explanation."

He frowned. "And you don't like me very much, do you?"

"I don't really know you well enough to have an opinion." She dropped her napkin on the table. "I must be going back."

"I'll walk you to your car," he said. He paid the bill, and she thanked him for the lunch as they walked outside.

"My pleasure," he said. "Even if you did cop my pie."

She smiled. "I definitely owe you a piece of pecan pie."

"And I intend to collect," he said, his voice low.

She glanced up at him quickly, but he was looking at the sky.

"It's gotten cloudy since we went into the restaurant," he said. "Chillier too. Don't you want to put that jacket on?"

"Yes, I think I will," she said. Now that her dress was dry.

He took the blazer from her and held it out so that she could slip her arms into the sleeves. He smoothed it over her shoulders, then his hands lingered for a seemingly endless moment. The honey-colored heat from his touch poured through Mallory, and she was unable to speak as Michael circled her shoulders with his arm.

"Where's your car?" he asked.

"Around the side," she said, praying her voice was steady. "The front lot was full when I came."

He nodded and they walked along the sidewalk, Michael drawing her closer to his side. Mallory was acutely conscious of the strength of his arm, of the power in his body. The body that was so very close to hers . . . She even caught the aroma of a woodsy after-shave. The aura of masculinity emanating from Michael increased her awareness of her own femininity, and she felt strangely safe and protected as she walked close to him.

"There it is," she said, pointing to her car.

"It's blue? Last night it was a weird shade of pea soup."

And Michael had been orange, she thought, smiling. "It was the lights in the parking lot at the police station."

"Such an auspicious first meeting we had," he said, chuckling softly as they stopped by her car.

"Indeed. Well, thank you again and—"

"Mallory," he interrupted, cradling her face in his hands, "I'm going to kiss you now."

She swallowed heavily. "Pardon me?"

"I know you said that kisses shouldn't be discussed before they happen, but I thought I'd warn you that I'm about to kiss you."

"In the parking lot?" she asked, her voice unnaturally high.

"I'm crazy about kissing beautiful women in parking lots," he said, and slowly lowered his head.

He brushed his lips over hers, then slid his tongue along her lower lip. She gasped at the delicious feeling, and he took her mouth, seeking and gaining entry to the sweet darkness within. She lifted her arms to circle his neck, inching her fingers into his thick hair. The kiss intensified. Tongues dueled in lazy, seductive circles, and a pulsing sensation began deep within Mallory.

The color of fire, her mind whispered. Michael's kiss was a consuming flame of hot, swirling desire. It was sweeping through her, igniting her passion as it went. Her breasts ached with a strange heaviness, and her knees began to tremble.

"Mallory," Michael said when his lips finally left hers, "I think I'd better stop kissing you now. Right now!"

"What?" she murmured dreamily.

"Mallory, we're in a parking lot!"

"Oh, good Lord," she said, taking a wobbly step backward.

He caught her hands and brought each to his mouth, kissing the palms. Mallory shivered.

"That was quite a kiss, Miss Carson," he said, his voice raspy. "Incredible, in fact. Would you be offended if I tore off all your clothes and made love to you on the top of your car?"

Not at all, she thought. It sounded like a fantastic idea. "I'll pass," she said, smiling at him.

He opened the door for her. "I'll talk with you soon," he said.

She slid into the car. "About our mothers."

"Among other things."

He closed the door, and it took every ounce of Mallory's concentration to insert her key in the ignition, then to drive out of the parking lot. When she glanced in the rearview mirror, Michael was standing perfectly still, watching her leave. It was only after she was a full block from the restaurant that she drew a deep, unsteady breath.

The kiss, she thought, that she had shared with Michael Patterson had melted her right down to her stockinged toes. It had been like nothing she had ever experienced before. It had boggled her mind and thrown her body into a tailspin.

Michael Patterson was one helluva kisser! And he was a very dangerous man.

When held in his arms, with his lips and tongue working their magic, she had wanted Michael, had wanted to make love with a man she hardly knew. Saints above, what was happening to her? She did not indulge in casual sex. She also didn't kiss the living daylights out of a man in a busy parking lot. But she'd done it, all right. She'd molded herself to Michael's body like Super Glue and returned his kiss with shocking abandon. And how absolutely fabulous that kiss had been!

"Don't think about it," she said aloud. "Forget it ever happened." Ha! Who was she kidding?

At the Honey Bee all was quiet as the children took their afternoon naps. Mallory entered her office and sank onto the chair behind her desk with a weary sigh.

"Have a nice lunch?" a woman asked, peering around the door.

"Hi, Patty," Mallory said. "Yes, lunch was pleasant, although no miraculous solution to the problem was produced."

"The Mighty Moms," Patty said, laughing. She came into the office and sat down in the chair opposite Mallory's desk. "I still feel they're just going through a stage, like kids do. What does Mary Louise's son think?"

"Michael isn't sure what they're up to. We're doing a waiting and watching number for a while."

"I thought his name was Mikey."

Mallory laughed. "Only to Mary Louise. Believe me, Patty, that man is not a Mikey."

"Oh? Sounds interesting. Is he good-looking?"

"Gorgeous."

"Really?" Patty said, sitting up straighter in her chair. "Do you think he'd be interested in a thirty-two-year-old divorcée with a four-year-old son? Said woman being only twenty pounds overweight and in need of a nose job. Said woman, of course, being me."

"There's nothing wrong with your nose."

"It's lumpy, but then, so is my body. Forget it. I was married to a gorgeous man. My next husband is going to be ugly as sin. That reduces the risk of him playing around. What does gorgeous Michael do?"

"He's a divorce lawyer. He also has a background in psychology, which he uses to help his clients whenever possible."

"Oh, ugh, really forget it. I'd never be able to hide the fact that I'm slightly cuckoo from *him*. Michael is all yours, Mallory. Go with my blessings."

"I'm not intending to 'go' anywhere with Michael Patterson," Mallory said. Only to bed, her mind whispered. "No!"

"Hey," Patty said. "I didn't mean to upset you."

"I'm sorry, I'm just tired. I'm beginning to think that my whirlwind social life is getting to be a bit much. Besides, racing to the police station in the middle of the night wreaks havoc with one's sleeping program. Speaking of which, I assume all our little darlings are snoozing?"

"Yep. Well, resting anyway. I hope it doesn't rain. They're so wild when we have to keep them in for hours. Makes for a long day."

"And then you still have the evening ahead with Andy," Mallory said, frowning.

"That's for sure. Where he gets all his energy I'll never know. We go home, eat, then it's bath time, story or game, then ten drinks of water before he finally conks out."

"While I just lock up here and go home to a quiet apartment or a night on the town."

"Oh-h-h," Patty moaned. "That sounds heavenly. No, I'm kidding. I can't imagine my life without Andy. His father was a louse, but I got a neat kid out of the deal. Of course, there are days when I wish motherhood wasn't a twenty-four-hour-a-day career. You're probably the smart one, Mallory. You're a mommy all day, and your own person at night."

"Michael said something like that at lunch. I don't know, Patty. That makes me sound rather self-centered, as though I don't become emotionally involved with these children so that I'll have all my stamina left for the fun evening ahead."

"I don't think it's self-centered," Patty said, shrugging. "You have an exciting, busy life-style, that's all. Marriage and babies apparently don't fit into your scheme of things. There's nothing terrible about that. Well, I'll go set out the glasses for the juice."

"I'll be there in a minute," Mallory said weakly.

"No rush," Patty said, and left the room.

Mallory pressed trembling hands to her aching temples. First Michael, and now Patty, she thought. Well, they were wrong. She *did* want children of her own, and a husband to love. Didn't she? Yes, of course, she did. But what had Michael said? That he and she put their professional concerns on a mental shelf at the end of the day, and didn't think about them again until morning? He didn't walk in the shoes of a wife-beater . . . and she didn't walk in the shoes of a mother.

Damn that Michael Patterson! It had all been so clear in her mind, so picture-perfect. She'd marry the man of her dreams, have their baby, and when the child was old enough, bring him or her to the Honey Bee every day. She would have the best of both worlds—a loving family and a rewarding career. But what did she know, really know, about it all? She'd never been in love and, heaven help her, she'd never been a mother. She was playing at motherhood with other women's children.

Had she ever taken care of a sick child? she asked herself. No, the mothers kept them home when they were ill. While Patty was bathing a rambunctious Andy, Mallory was lounging in a bubble bath sipping a glass of white wine. As she dressed in an elegant gown to attend a black-tie party, Patty was probably reading *The Three Little Pigs* to a wiggling bundle of boy on her lap.

Dear heaven, she was falling apart, Mallory thought as tears burned her eyes. She was suddenly so unsure of herself and her future. What sort of game had she been playing with herself? Had she subconsciously found fault with the men who had hinted at more serious, committed relationships? Had they really been unsuitable, or had she simply found a way to postpone yet again her plans for a husband and children?

Why didn't she know herself better than this?

Who was she? What was she afraid of? What did she really want to do with her life? So many questions, questions that hadn't been there before she had sat across the table from Michael. He had seen something in her, sensed something that she, herself, didn't know existed. He had gazed at her with his fathomless dark eyes, and somehow had found the path to her soul. What was he doing to her well-ordered life and serene existence?

Oh, damn that Michael Patterson!

Three

Mallory arrived early at the Honey Bee the next morning. She wandered from room to room, not really seeing the bookcases filled with toys and books, the bright, child-size furniture, the rows of neatly made up cots in the Snoozing Room. Large cardboard bees smiled at her from the walls, but they did not cheer her.

She had spent the evening at home last night, a rare occurrence for her. And during those long, seemingly endless hours she had mulled over what Michael had said at lunch, and what she wanted from life.

She could see why Michael, a divorce lawyer, needed to perfect the ability to mentally shelve the events of his day. He dealt in people's shattered dreams, shattered lives, even. For him not to be able to put all of that away when he left the office would be neither healthy nor wise. She could understand his approach to his demanding and draining career.

But what about herself? How did she justify holding herself back from innocent children? Was it simply mechanical when she hugged them, soothed their tears, shared their laughter? Didn't she know how to truly give of herself, truly love?

Mallory sighed, feeling tired, both emotionally and physically. She probably needed a vacation, but didn't dare take one now. There was no telling what gruesome trouble Clarissa and Mary Louise might get into with one of their wardens off duty. She and Michael had to watch them like hawks.

Michael . . .

At that moment the front door opened, and three children raced in, calling hello gleefully. With a weary smile Mallory went to greet them. The day at the Honey Bee had begun.

Two hours later Mallory was bending over a low table, helping a little girl paste a lopsided house made of construction paper onto a large sheet of butcher paper. The project was a huge mural to be hung on the wall, and each of the four-year-olds was adding his or her special touch. Patty had wailed in dismay when Andy had made a very round figure, declaring it to be his mommy.

"Mallory?" her secretary said, poking her head in the door. "Telephone."

"Thanks, Denise," Mallory said. She quickly washed the paste from her hands, dried them on a paper towel, and headed for her office. "I'll be right back, Patty."

"No problem," Patty said. "Andy and I are going to have an in-depth discussion as to how he views his voluptuous mother. Jason, do not color Sally's nose. Stay on the paper, young man."

In her office Mallory snatched up the telephone receiver and said hello.

"Mallory?" a deep voice replied.

Michael! she thought, and her breath caught..

"This is Michael Patterson."

She knew that. She knew his voice, his taste, his aroma. . . . "Hello, Michael," she said, sinking onto her chair.

"I just thought I'd warn you," he said, chuckling softly. "You're getting company."

"Company?"

"Mary Louise Patterson and Clarissa Carson are descending upon the Honey Bee to take pictures of the children for their book."

"Oh, no."

"Oh, yes. I just called Mother and caught her as she was leaving the house on her way to collect Clarissa."

"Wonderful," Mallory muttered. "I need this like I need a toothache."

"Cheer up. It could be worse."

"I doubt it. How, pray tell, could it be worse?"

"They're coming in my mother's car, not on the back of Snake and Jake's motorcycles."

"That's cute, Michael. Just too cute for words."

He laughed. "Stay alert, partner," he said. "See what info you can pick up, any clues, you know what I mean? We need the inside scoop on this caper, sweetheart."

"If that was supposed to be Humphrey Bogart," Mallory said, laughing, "it didn't quite make it."

"No, huh? Oh, well. Listen, if you're free, why don't we have dinner tonight so you can fill me in on whatever you find out from the Terrible Twosome of Tucson. Seven o'clock?"

She frowned as she studied her calender. She *did* have a date this evening, but only for drinks. She could be home by . . . "How about seven-thirty?" she asked.

"That's fine. How about if I pick up a pizza and bring it to your place? Are you in the book?"

"Yes, apartment two ten."

"Great. See you then. Oh, and good luck."

"Thanks," she said dryly.

"And, Mallory? I'm looking forward to seeing you again. Wear your hair down, would you? Bye."

"Good-bye," she said to the dial tone, and replaced the receiver. Wear her hair down? she repeated silently. What gall! That was a crummy, sexist thing for Michael to have said. How would he have liked it if she'd told him to come without a shirt? Now *there* was an enticing thought. Oh, for Pete's sake.

"Hello, hello," her mother called, bouncing into the office with Mary Louise at her heels.

"My, my, what a surprise," Mallory said, trying to sound surprised. "To what do I owe this honor, ladies?"

"We want to take pictures of the children for our book," Clarissa said.

"Mother, I'm not sure you can use photos of people without their permission. Have you checked all this out with your lawyer?"

"I never thought of that," Clarissa said, squinting at the ceiling. "We might get our pants sued off."

"You're being graphic again," Mallory said, getting to her feet.

"Mikey will be terribly upset with me if I get sued," Mary Louise said. "He'll rant and rave for days."

"So will I," Mallory said.

"Well," Clarissa said brightly, "we'll just halt production until we check with my legal eagle. But as long as we're here, we could help you with the children."

"Good idea," Mary Louise said.

"You wouldn't rather go right over to the attorney's?" Mallory asked. "I mean, after all, this book is your top priority, right?"

"It is?" Clarissa said. "Oh, yes, of course, it is. But you look rather tired, Mallory. It's my duty as a mother to help my child whenever possible. Come along, Mary Louise. Let's see what the babies are up to. Oh, I hope that little Jeffy is here today. He just melts my heart when he smiles at me."

As the two women bustled out the door, Mallory sank back onto the edge of her desk. That book of theirs was a con! she thought. They didn't care diddly if it ever got published. Their mission at the Honey Bee this morning was to play with the children, no doubt about it. Michael had been right. Clarissa and Mary Louise were bored—*and* they wanted to be grandmothers. Oh, they had a dream all right, but it wasn't a book with their names on the cover. It was weddings, then baby showers. But how far did their fantasy go? Did it include the wedded bliss of Mallory Carson and Michael Patterson? Or would they settle for their offspring marrying anyone as long as the sought-after grandchildren were produced? Interesting. Very interesting. Well, she certainly had a newsflash to report to Michael that night.

Michael, she mused. He was coming to her apartment to share a pizza dinner. No big deal. She could handle it. Oh, really? Could she, who had plastered herself to him and kissed him senseless in a parking lot, behave herself while in her apartment alone with Michael? Of course, she could. She wasn't some kind of wanton hussy. She'd give him her report, stuff him full of pizza, and send him on his way. Fine.

The day passed quickly at the Honey Bee. The children adored Clarissa and Mary Louise, and Mallory couldn't help but smile at the rapport between old and young.

"The mothers are wonderful," Patty said to Mallory in the middle of the afternoon. "Thanks to them, I won't go home thoroughly exhausted tonight. Maybe I'll take Andy out to dinner as a special treat."

"Why don't you hire a baby-sitter and take *yourself* out to dinner as a special treat?" Mallory asked. "See a movie afterward."

"That wouldn't be fair," Patty said. "Andy deserves to reap the rewards of a mother who isn't out on her feet. We'll have fun. I'm going to give Clarissa and Mary Louise a big smooch when they leave. They're so patient with the kids."

"Yes, they'd make marvelous grandmothers," Mallory said quietly.

"Well, maybe ol' Mikey will come through. You know, marry some gal and have a slew of little Mikeys."

"Aren't I eligible to produce a grandchild?" Mallory asked, frowning.

"Oh, well sure," Patty said, shrugging. "But I figure you have your life set up the way you want it."

"Playing mommy during the day, and having my evenings for whatever I choose," Mallory said, a knot tightening in her stomach.

"Right. Oops, Kevin spilled his juice. I'll take care of it. A mother's work is never done," she added as she hurried away.

A real mother's work, Mallory thought dismally. A pretend mother, a playing-at-it mother, locked the door at six o'clock and walked away.

At seven-twenty that evening Mallory rushed into her apartment. She tossed her bag and jacket on the sofa and hurried into the bedroom. There she snatched up a clean pair of designer jeans and a royal-blue cashmere sweater, and quickly changed. She brushed out her hair until it was a raven cascade tumbling past her shoulders. She recalled Michael's firm directive to wear her hair down, then began to twist it into a bun. In the next instant she hesitated, and allowed the thick tresses to fall free again.

"Oh, what the heck, why not?" she said to her reflection. She might as well admit she'd chosen to wear the blue sweater because it did marvelous things for her eyes, and she knew the expensive jeans were snug in all the right places. She had dressed for Michael, so why not wear her hair the way he liked it? No sense in playing games about the whole thing.

Games. Playing games. There it was again, the source of her confusion and misery. Somehow, somewhere she had lost herself, Mallory Carson, in the shuffle. Did she really want a husband and child? Did she? Or was she actually quite content with her life exactly as it was? And, damn it, why didn't she know?

She walked back into the living room and began quickly picking up the newspapers and magazines that were strewn across it. She had just hung her jacket in the closet when a knock sounded at the door. She opened it to a smiling Michael Patterson.

"Pizza delivery," he said as he stepped into the apartment. "It's still hot, believe it or not. Hungry?"

"Definitely," she said, closing the door. "Oh, it smells delicious."

"That bag under my arm has beer and soda. I didn't know which you wanted."

"Pizza and beer. Perfect. Follow me, Mr. Patterson."

"Anywhere, Miss Carson," he said in a low voice. "You don't even have to blow in my ear."

She laughed, ignoring the shiver that was dancing along her spine, and waved Michael toward the dining room as she went into the kitchen for glasses and napkins. Okay, she told herself. So Michael was fabulous in faded jeans and a dark brown sweater that made his shoulders appear a block wide. And, yes, his tawny hair was thick and seemed to be calling to her to run her fingers through it. And she was willing to admit that her breathing was slightly unsteady because he looked and smelled just so darn good. But so what?

"Michael," she called, "I have a news flash for you."

"And I have one for you," he said, directly behind her.

She spun around and collided with the hard wall of his chest. She slowly lifted her head to look up at him as his strong arms enfolded her.

"I didn't know you were here," she said, her voice trembling. "I mean, I thought you were out there."

"I had to deliver *my* news flash."

"Oh. What is it?"

"I'm going to kiss you again. I realize I'm discussing it, and you think that's dumb, but in this case it's necessary."

"It is?" she said, and swallowed heavily.

"It is. You see. I want to tell you *why* I'm going to kiss you again. It's because that kiss we shared in the parking lot was incredible. You feel like heaven in my arms, Mallory Carson, and kissing you is like tasting the nectar of a beautiful flower. I suppose that sounds corny, but it's true, every word. I've relived that kiss over and over, and now I need another one to replenish my memory bank. And so, I'm going to kiss you . . . for a very long time."

"Oh-h-h, good Lord," she whispered, going nearly limp in his arms. "That was the dearest, most lovely bunch of bull I've ever heard. Kiss me, Michael. You've convinced me it's a terrific idea."

"I meant every word," he said, lowering his head. "Every single word."

His mouth melted over hers as she stood on tiptoe to circle his neck with her arms. A soft sigh of pleasure escaped her, and he answered by gently parting her lips and easing his tongue into her mouth.

At first the kiss was the color of smoke and smoldering embers, until the embers burst into the flame of heated passion. Michael's hands roamed over Mallory's back, then slid to her buttocks to fit her more tightly to him. His arousal was hard against her, evidence of his desire for her. He groaned deep in his chest, and the kiss went on and on.

A coiling knot of need burned deep within Mallory. As their tongues mated in a rhythmic dance, her breasts ached to be touched by Michael's strong but gentle hands. She felt a tremor of desire sweep through his body, and leaned closer to him, pressing herself against him.

"Mallory," he gasped, tearing his mouth from hers. "Lord, I want you. I want you so damn much."

"Yes," she said dreamily, then an instant later, "No! What am I doing?"

"Kissing me," he said, not releasing his hold on her. "And wanting me to make love with you. You do want me, Mallory, I know you do."

"I know I do too," she said, flattening her hands on his chest, "but I'm not going to have sex with you."

"No, we're not going to have casual sex, we're going to make love. There's a big difference between the two."

"Semantics, Michael."

"The emotional level of caring, Mallory."

She pulled back against his arms and he let her go. "That," she said, "coming from the man who puts his emotions on a mental shelf at will?"

His jaw tightened slightly. "I was referring to my work when I said that. You should understand about putting your job away at day's end. You do the same thing."

"Yes, I guess I have to admit that I do," she said quietly.

"And it has nothing to do with us, as a man and a woman, wanting each other. There's something terrific happening between us, Mallory. You can't deny that."

"Yes, okay, so I want you," she said, her voice rising. "But I don't know why! Is this good old-fashioned lust? Or is it something else? Something new and special? Something I've never experienced before? I don't know. And do you know why I don't know? Because nothing in my life makes sense to me right now. Nothing! Ever since I met you, because of the things you've said and done, I've become a befuddled mess."

"I don't understand," he said, running his hand over the back of his neck. "Things *I've* said and done? What things?"

"Oh, Michael. It's all so complicated and . . . and the pizza is getting cold."

"Hey," he said, stepping closer to her and weaving his fingers through her hair. "Talk to me. You're obviously upset, and I'm somehow to blame."

"No, you're not," she said, looking up at him. "Not really. I've been playing games with myself. Then you said . . . Then Patty said . . . Then I knew I wasn't being honest about . . . Now I don't even know what I truly want. See? I told you I was a befuddled mess."

He shook his head. "I didn't understand a word of what you just said."

"Some psychologist-lawyer you are," she said, managing a weak smile.

"I *thought* I was good. I sure charge a helluva lot. But you've got me totally baffled, kid."

"Oh, well," she said, throwing up her hands. "I'll figure it all out. I think. I hope. I have to!"

"In the meantime," he said, grinning at her, "let's make love."

"No, let's reheat the pizza in the microwave."

"I had a feeling we weren't going to make love. Where's that beer? I've earned a drink. I deserve and demand a drink."

Mallory laughed, pulled two plates from the cupboard, and shoved them into Michael's hands. He carried them out to the dining room. He was so warm and caring and fun, she mused. It had been very unfair of her to blurt out that her mental dilemma was his fault. But he hadn't gotten angry, he had sincerely wanted to help her. He also could have accused her of being a tease after kissing him the way she had, then calling a halt before it went further. But he hadn't. He was sweet, understanding, and lovable. Lovable? The kind of man she could fall in love with?

Good Lord, no! That was the last thing she needed at the moment, she told herself. She didn't even know if she *wanted* to fall in love. And if she did want to, Michael was the wrong man. Marriage was as appealing as the plague to him. If her future did include a husband and children, the man in the picture was not Michael Patterson.

The pizza was bubbly-hot when Mallory brought it to the dining room table. She sat down opposite Michael and smiled at him.

"How macho," she said. "You drink your beer right from the can."

"Like that? Well, shucks, darlin'," he drawled, "wait 'til y'all see me crush this can in my bare hand."

"Spare me," she said, laughing as she picked up a large gooey slice of pizza. "Oh, this looks good."

"I'm a great pizza deliverer. Mallory, I really wish you'd tell me what I did to upset you."

She shook her head as she took a bite of the pizza.

"No, huh?" He frowned. "Well, let me think here. I barked at you at the police station, but I apologized for that. I called your mother a jailbird, but admitted that mine was one too. We had a nice lunch, I pointed out how much we have in common, I said you were beautiful, you stole my pecan pie. The kiss in the parking lot! That's it, right? You think I've blown your reputation because I kissed you in the parking lot of a restaurant."

"No."

"Oh. Well, that's good, because it was a terrific kiss. Second only to the kiss in the kitchen. So what did I leave out?"

"Nothing. Michael, please, I'm really sorry I acted the way I did. I just have a lot on my mind, and none of it is your fault, not really. I need to sort through some things, that's all."

"Well, I'm here if you want to talk. Okay? That's not psychologist-lawyer Patterson speaking. It's me, Michael, who likes you very much, Mallory Carson."

"Thank you," she said.

Their gazes met for a long moment, a sharing moment, then Mallory averted her eyes and poured her beer into the glass. Michael was so nice, she mused. What color was nice? Pink. Soft, fuzzy pink, like a favorite blanket or a teddy bear. Michael Patterson a teddy bear? Not quite. He was big, and strong, and tightly muscled, like a fine racehorse. And he was power and authority, moving with assurance like a sleek panther. No, with his gorgeous, sun-streaked hair he was a lion, the king of the jungle, the—

"Mallory?"

"What?" she said, jumping slightly.

"Can you come back from wherever you are, and tell me your news flash about the Gruesome Twosome?"

"Oh, yes, the mothers. Michael, the book is a smoke screen, I'm sure of it. They said they came to the Honey Bee to take pictures of the children, and I mentioned they might need releases to use people's photographs. Instead of dashing to the attorney's, they spent the day playing with the kids. I'm convinced that's why they came in the first place. When they left, I had to run out to their car and give them their cameras."

"The book is not their dream?"

"No, I really don't think so. You were right, they're bored. And after watching the two of them with the children, I think they're longing for grandchildren. My mother has stopped by before, but never spent the entire day like that."

"Did they get in the way?"

"Heavens, no. They were a tremendous help. It made a big difference in how tired we were by the end of the day. I assured both Clarissa and Mary Louise that they were welcome to come any time. My staff will roll out the red carpet for them."

"Grandchildren," Michael said, frowning. "Wonderful. What are we supposed to do? Order them a couple from the Sears catalog?"

"That's a thought. The only piece to the puzzle that is still missing is whether or not they're matchmaking, scheming to get you and me together. There was no hint of that today, so I don't know. Have you ever explained your views on marriage to Mary Louise?"

"Yeah," he said gruffly. "She said I needed a pyscyologist."

"Oh." Mallory smiled. "Sort of like, 'Physician heal thyself'?"

"Something like that. She certainly didn't understand where I was coming from on the subject."

"Well, you said your parents had a very happy marriage."

"They did, but in another era—with less pressure, less stress. Men and women of today are coping with a different type of society from the one our folks did. Everything is geared up to the maximum. A man or a woman is expected to throw himself or herself body and soul into work, then go home and meet the needs of another person. That's not even close to realistic. I suppose I sound rather selfish saying these things, but I feel I'm facing the facts head-on. I don't want to marry someone, then continually fall short in my role of husband, friend, source of comfort and encouragement."

"But you said you put your work on a mental shelf before you go home."

"I do, to a point. But it's still draining, still takes its toll. I couldn't start in solving the problems of my family the minute I walked in the door. We're getting off the subject, Mallory, and I'm getting on my soapbox. Back to the mothers. Okay, the book is a smoke screen, as you said. They want grandchildren. We don't know if they're hell-bent on seeing you and me riding off into the sunset together. It's not such a bad situation."

"It's not?"

"No. They can go to the Honey Bee and play with the kids since you've told them they're welcome there. That should satisfy their maternal urges for a while at least. We'll stay alert for any signs that they're trying to get us together. We're one step ahead of them now. We've got it made."

"Do you really think so?"

"Yep. They'll have to give up sooner or later. Unless, of course, you marry someone."

"Me? Oh, well, I . . . well . . ."

"Is there a candidate in the wings?" he asked, looking at her steadily.

"No."

"I'm surprised. Not sorry, you understand, but definitely surprised. I would have thought some guy would have snatched you up by now. You're a beautiful, intelligent, desirable woman."

Tack on *confused* and *frightened*, Mallory thought. "Nope," she said breezily. "I'm footloose and fancy-free."

"I'm very glad to hear that," he said, his voice seeming to drop an octave. "Then there's no reason why we can't see each other, right?"

"I'm not sure that's a good idea, Michael. The mothers might get all excited about nothing."

"They don't have to know."

"Well, it would avoid a lot of hassle if they didn't realize we were going out together."

"Then you agree that we should see each other?"

"Well, I—I'm not sure, Michael. I don't seem to behave to form around you. It's rather disturbing."

"What is? The fact that we've shared some fantastic kisses? The fact that you want me as much as I want you? That's disturbing?"

"Yes! It certainly is."

"Why?"

"Because I normally move very slowly in a relationship. I don't go leaping into men's arms in parking lots and kitchens. And heaven knows I don't entertain ideas about— Why am I having this conversation with you?"

He smiled. "Who else are you going to have it with?" He captured her hand in his. "We're talking about us, and where we go from here."

"Well, it won't be into the bedroom!" she said, slipping her hand free.

"You wound me," he exclaimed. "Do you think I'm only after your body?"

"No," she said, bursting into laughter. "I'm worried that I'm after yours!"

He grinned. "Sounds good to me. Should I take off my clothes now?"

"Oh, Michael." She sighed. "I don't know what to do. You could have accused me of being a tease after what happened in the kitchen. I'm really very confused right now about a great many things. Maybe it would be best if we didn't see each other again."

"Hey, not fair. You can't dust me off, I just found you. Look, I'm not going to rush you. I won't seduce the hell out of you and drag you into bed. Nothing is going to happen between us that you aren't ready for. I do intend to kiss you a helluva lot, though. I like kissing you, Mallory Carson. It's high on my list of fantastic things to do. Right up there with watching pro football and eating peanut butter—and—mayonnaise sandwiches."

"My goodness," she said, teasing. "I rank as high as peanut butter and mayonnaise?"

"Yep, and I don't go around saying that to every woman I meet."

"I'm honored, sir."

"You should be. Want that last piece of pizza?"

"No, go ahead. Did you play football?"

"One year in college. I got my leg broken under a pile of humanity, and that was that. Now I enjoy racquetball, running, and swimming. Mary Louise gave me a set of golf clubs because, according to her, lawyers are supposed to play golf. Man, I hate that game. It's so slow."

"And you are a zoomer. I noticed that about you right away."

"A zoomer? Have I been insulted? Actually I can be very patient when the occasion calls for it."

"Well, yes, I'm sure that some divorce cases are very tedious and complicated."

"I wasn't referring to my work. I was talking

about you, us. For some reason I think you've pegged me as a hustler, and I'm going to prove to you that you're wrong. We'll move at a nice, slow, easy pace. You have no reason to be frightened of me, or of yourself for that matter, and you'll come to realize that."

"You sound awfully sure of yourself."

"No, just determined. You knock me over by just responding to my kisses, Mallory. The thought of us making love absolutely blows my mind. We are going to be so damn good together, and it's definitely worth waiting for."

"Oh, is that so?" she said, glaring at him. "I don't recall agreeing to make love with you somewhere down the road."

"All in good time, darlin'," he said, grinning as he pulled the tab on another beer. "All in good time."

"Now, look, Michael, I—"

"Did you notice," he interrupted, "that you referred to our coming together as making love, not having casual sex?"

"So?"

"So, we're doing just fine, we really are. Say, you don't have any pecan pie hiding in your kitchen, do you?"

Four

After haughtily telling Michael no, she did not have any pecan pie, Mallory carried their dishes and the empty pizza box into the kitchen. When she returned, Michael had wandered into the living room and was standing with his back to her. His hands were shoved into his jean pockets as he examined the books on the packed shelves against the far wall. Despite the distance between them, she could sense the power in his body, the raw sexuality he exuded. It seemed to reach out to her, to stroke her, causing her pulse to skitter.

What would it be like to make love—not have sex—with Michael? she wondered, and knew the answer immediately. It would be fabulous, a joining not just of the bodies, but of the minds and souls as well. And therein lay the danger. How easy it would be to fall in love with Michael, a man who never wanted to marry!

Still, he was irresistible, and she crossed the room to him as if drawn by an unbreakable silken cord. Standing near him, inhaling his special aroma, feeling the heat emanating from his hard body, she had to struggle to resist touching him.

He turned and smiled at her. "You have quite a few books," he said. "And quite a variety."

She glanced at her shelves, which held all sorts of books from biographies to suspense novels, many of them hardcover editions, and shrugged. "I like to read."

"And these." He walked over to two paintings hanging on the wall to the right. "These are original oils, aren't they?"

She gazed at the paintings and smiled, as she always did when she looked at them. One was a vase of flowers, a riotous explosion of color. The other was of a canal in Venice in the springtime. The sunlight that reflected off the elegant buildings and the water was so bright, so clear, the painting itself seemed to glow.

"Yes, they're originals," she said. "I got them in Europe. It was difficult shipping them home, but well worth it. I fell in love with both paintings when I first saw them."

He studied her face. "You know, some people would own paintings like this just to prove they had enough money and sense to collect art. But you obviously care more for the beauty of it than the prestige."

"Oh, yes." She turned to him. "While I was growing up, my mother taught me that my father had worked very hard, and because of that we were left with the means to live . . . well, more than comfortably. But she always stressed that we mustn't take any of it for granted, and should have pride in not only our possessions, but in the way we live our lives."

"I like that," Michael said. "And it matches up with what you said about the Honey Bee. You had the money to get it started, but it was your hard work and determination that made it a success."

"Yes."

He nodded and his gaze swept over the living room.

"This really is a nice place," he said. "Bright, cheerful, uncluttered. It has your touch, your style. Understated but classy. My mother has doodads all over the place. Drives me nuts."

"That's me all right," Mallory said quietly. "Uncluttered."

"Hey, don't sound so sad," he said, smiling down at her. "I take it you're now referring to your life. Is that such a bad way to live?"

"I don't know. Let's not get started on the subject of me and my life again. I really don't want to talk about it."

"Got it." He walked over to the sofa and sat down. "Come here," he said, patting the cushion next to him.

"Would you care for some brandy?"

"After pizza and beer? No, thanks. Come here."

"Shall I turn on the stereo?"

"Go right ahead, but what will you do after that? Decide to wash the kitchen floor? You're definitely avoiding sitting close to me."

"You're right."

"Well," he said, spreading his arms out along

the back of the sofa, "I suppose I could come back over there and stand by you, but eventually our feet would start to hurt. Why don't you just plunk your cute tush next to me here?"

"And?"

He shrugged. "And we can either talk about the weather, or I'll tear off all your clothes and jump on your bones, whichever suits your fancy. I aim to please."

She laughed, then walked over to the sofa and sat down. "So okay," she said, "I'm acting ridiculous."

"*Cautious* is a better word," he said, smiling. "Don't be so hard on yourself."

"Michael, have you always been so—oh, I don't know—so secure, so sure of yourself? Have you always known who you were, what you wanted and didn't want?"

He frowned. "Is that how you see me?"

"Well, yes."

"Were those polite phrases for *arrogant* and *cocky*?"

"I don't think so," she said, smiling. "You just seem to have total control of your life."

"Oh, I've been known to lose it now and then. I don't like it, but it does happen. I am human, you know. I make mistakes, I have to pull back, regroup, start over. I don't care for that because it slows me down. I don't have much patience with myself."

"Yet you accept the failings in the people who seek your professional help."

"True," he said, nodding. "But it's a proven fact that we're often our own worst enemies. When I get off the track, I get very frustrated and angry. I really give myself hell."

"That's not very nice," Mallory said, frowning. "Shouldn't you be your own best friend? Anyway, what would you do if you discovered that you were no longer sure of the plan you'd made for your life? Started questioning your outlook, your opinions, your goals, wondering if they were still what you wanted?"

"I wouldn't allow that to happen," he said bluntly. "Lord, Mallory, I'm thirty-six years old. I sure as hell better have my act together by now, know exactly who I am and where I'm going, or I'd be in a pretty sorry place."

"But people do change."

"*I* don't. I wouldn't pull the rug out from under myself at this point in my life. My program is set. End of story."

"But you said no one is too old to have a dream."

"I don't have any dreams," he said, lifting a shoulder in a shrug. "I have everything I need."

But what about love? she wondered. Wasn't there even a minute section within Michael that yearned to love and be loved in return? To be half of a glorious whole, sharing, laughing, crying with someone? Didn't he ever get lonely moving through life as he did?

"Hey," he said, slipping his hand to the nape of her neck. "You've gone away again. You are one heavy-duty thinker, Mallory."

"Oh, sorry. I was just mulling over what you said. You're a complicated man, Michael."

"You've *got* to be kidding," he said, laughing. "I don't see myself that way at all. I'm on a straight, clear-cut path from here to there, no detours, no passing go and collecting two hundred dollars."

"No changes," she said softly.

"Nope. And, please don't say that to change is to grow. I'm all grown up, and doing fine. Is there a specific reason for this conversation, or are we chatting?"

"What? Oh, I'm just trying to understand you, get to know you better, I guess."

"That's the best news I've had all day. Mallory Carson wants to get to know me better. Well, you've examined my brain. Want to start in on my body?"

"No, thank you," she said, smiling. "Nice of you to offer though."

"Any time. Listen, how would you like to handle the fact that I'm about to kiss you? Do you want me to announce it again, or just move in and get the job done?"

"Oh, good Lord," she said, rolling her eyes to the heavens.

"Just trying to cooperate," he said, leaning toward her. "Wouldn't want to upset you. But I really do need to kiss you, Mallory."

"I . . ."

"I really"—he brushed his lips over hers—"do."

The kiss was tentative at first, as though Michael were holding back, waiting for permission to proceed. But when she parted her lips, the kiss deepened as he slid his arm around her waist, his other hand still at the nape of her neck. She flattened her hands on his chest, then inched them upward, savoring the feel of his steely muscles. She circled his neck with her arms, running her fingers through his thick hair. His tongue stroked hers, then urged hers into his mouth, and she gasped and tightened her hold on him.

He leaned back, shifting his legs up onto the sofa and taking her with him, until she was lying on top of him, her breasts crushed against his chest. She could feel every inch of his tightly muscled body, could feel his arousal, hard and hot beneath her hips. A tremor of desire swept through him and he slid his hands under her sweater. The honey-colored warmth from his touch ignited her passion further, bringing a soft purr from her throat.

In a smooth, powerful motion, he rolled over so that she was underneath him. He gazed into her eyes as his hand skimmed up to her breast. The nipple tautened against her lacy bra as he flicked his thumb rhythmically across it. His lips trailed a heated path along the slender column of her neck to the wildly beating pulse at the base, then up again to drink of the sweetness of her mouth.

She savored each sensation that was rocketing through her, savored the near pain of passion. The hot, fiery color of Michael's kiss mixed with the ebony of his strength and the dusky blue of his gentleness. The colors melted, one into the next, and swirled Mallory away with them. Her hands were restless, seeking. She eagerly pushed his sweater up so that she could touch and caress the moist, hot skin beneath. He trembled at her feathery touch, and groaned deep in his chest.

"Mallory," he gasped, jerking his mouth from hers. He buried his face in the fragrant cloud of her hair as he strove for control.

She wanted this man, she thought feverishly. She wanted Michael to make love to her. She ached with the need for him. Such promise his magnificent body held, such gifts of ecstasy that could be hers. Never before had she felt so alive, so aware of her femininity. Desire thudded unrelentingly deep within her, matched by the wild beating of her heart.

"Oh, Michael," she whispered. "Michael . . ."

"Damn," he said hoarsely, then pushed himself off her. He sat up and leaned his elbows on his knees, rubbing his face with trembling hands.

Mallory struggled to sit up as well, then wrapped her arms around her drawn-up legs. As she drew a shaky breath she watched Michael anxiously, knowing he must be angry. She'd done it again. She'd responded to his kiss with shocking abandon, giving every indication she was agreeing to go further. Yet she had adamantly told Michael that she did not engage in casual sex. Her actions were not matching her words, and he was no doubt furious at her for leading him on. She deserved whatever scathing accusations he hurled at her.

The silence hung in the room like an oppressive shroud.

He stared at the ceiling for a long moment, then turned his head to look at her. She stiffened, preparing herself for what she knew was to come.

"I'm sorry," he said, his voice raspy.

"What?" she said, her eyes widening.

"I'm sorry, Mallory. I just blew the slow-and-easy-we're-doing-fine program straight to hell. I could say that I desire you more than any woman

I've ever met, which would be true, but it sounds so damn phony, I'm not going to say it. Lord." He shook his head. "When I start kissing you, I don't want to stop! I really am sorry."

"Oh, Michael, please don't say that. I feel guilty enough without you apologizing. I say one thing, then do the exact opposite. I was kissing you back, in case you didn't notice. I'm capable of using the word *no*, but it was the farthest thought from my mind. I wouldn't have been surprised if the next thing out of my mouth had been 'Take me, I'm yours!' I don't know what's happening to me."

He chuckled. " 'Take me, I'm yours'?" he repeated. "I didn't think people actually said that."

"The point is," she said, frowning, "my behavior in regard to you is upsetting."

"*Your* word. Mine is *fantastic*. We're back to doing fine."

"No, we're not."

"Yes, we are," he said, pushing himself to his feet. "And I'm getting out of here while that status is intact."

"But . . ."

"I'll let myself out." He bent down and brushed his lips over hers. "Good night."

"But . . ."

"Talk to you soon," he said, then strode to the door and was gone.

"But . . ." Mallory said again, staring at the closed door. "Well, hell! He doesn't let me get a word in edgewise." Had Michael been orange again? she wondered. No, he hadn't been rude. He'd apologized, for heaven's sake. That was sweet of him, especially when she was equally to blame for what had taken place. She'd done it again, darn it. He touched her; she melted. He kissed her; she totally dissolved. She'd wanted to make love with Michael Patterson.

Would she have done it? she asked herself, resting her forehead on her bent knees. Yes. But why? Why Michael? Why did *his* kiss and *his* touch cause her to throw caution to the wind, give so much of herself to him, and want even more? It seemed she was beleaguered by questions regarding every aspect of her life. She had to start finding some answers before she went out of her mind. Confusion was *not* fun.

She sighed and walked into the kitchen to clean up the debris from the pizza and beer dinner. Then she wandered aimlessly around the apartment, dismissing the ideas of watching television or reading a book. She felt edgy, unable to sit in one spot.

She missed Michael.

"Wonderful," she muttered. "Now I miss him. I'm going to bed."

A short time later she was lying in bed, staring into the darkness, the blankets pulled up to her chin. A single tear slid down her cheek, and she angrily brushed it away. Memories of Michael washed over her; his image so vivid, she felt as though she could reach out and gather him into her embrace. Desire for Michael was humming through her body, causing her to shift restlessly on the bed. The bed that was too big, too empty, too lonely.

Lonely. The word echoed in her mind, then settled in her heart like a heavy stone. She thought of the parties she'd attended in the past months, the dates she'd had to concerts, movies, dinners. The faces of her escorts were a blur, and she couldn't remember any evening that she had enjoyed as much as this one with Michael. She had played yet another game, convincing herself that her jam-packed social life was exciting and fulfilling. But now, in the solitude of her bedroom, she knew it wasn't true.

She was lonely.

Tonight Michael had filled her apartment with his vibrant masculinity, and filled the emptiness within her with his smile, his touch, his kiss. The colors of Michael had transformed her bleak existence to one of vividness, awareness, joy.

Suddenly it all came clear to Mallory. She had been deluding herself all these years. She didn't want to live her life alone—going to work, going out, and then coming home to an empty apartment. She wanted to love, to be loved. She simply hadn't yet found the right man.

Was Michael the right man? she wondered. No! she answered herself forcefully. Michael was very much the wrong man. True, she enjoyed being with him, talking with him, kissing him. . . . But he didn't want any part of love, marriage, forever and ever. No, Michael was not the right man.

She willed herself to relax, feeling as though she were split in two. Part of her was relieved that she had conquered her inner confusion as to who she was and what she wanted. But another part of her was wary, fearful that she was headed toward a devastating disaster in the form of Michael Patterson.

As she drifted off to sleep her last gloomy realization was that she missed him.

The next day at the Honey Bee, Mallory paid close attention to how the women on her staff interacted with the children. They were warm, affectionate, and had seemingly endless patience. They gave hugs, dried tears, lavished praise upon their young charges. Yet Mallory saw, for the first time, the quiet closeness between Patty and Andy. It was almost undiscernible, but it was there, that special bond.

With an inward sigh of relief Mallory understood she was not playing at being a mother. She was holding that extra measure of emotion in her heart for the child she would have someday. She was filling the needs of these children until they could rush into their mothers' arms at day's end.

That night Mallory had dinner with two longtime friends, Becky and Janice, both married and with one child each. It was a pleasant evening, but strange. Mallory found herself quizzing her two friends about their babies, what an average day was like, how much their husbands were involved in taking care of the children. Becky and Janice finally refused to utter one more word on the subject, declaring this to be their night away from motherhood. They then turned the tables on Mallory, demanding to know why she was suddenly so interested in the world of bottles and diaper rash.

"It has to be a man," Becky said. "Spill the

beans, Mallory. Who is charging up your maternal instincts?"

"Don't be silly," Mallory said, feeling the warm blush on her cheeks. "I'm merely expressing an interest in your lives."

"Pooh!" Janice said. "You were a lousy liar in high school, and you still are. What's his name?"

"Pecan pie," Mallory said.

"What?"

"That's what I'm having for dessert, pecan pie."

Becky and Janice threw up their hands in defeat and changed the subject. And Mallory thought about Michael. While she ate her pecan pie, which she knew he would have enjoyed, she thought of Michael. As she drove home she thought of Michael. As she walked across the parking lot to her apartment she thought of Michael.

And there he was.

She gasped as Michael pushed himself away from her door and crossed his arms over his chest.

"Nice of you to drop by," he said gruffly as she neared him. "Do you realize it's after ten?"

"We didn't have plans together," she said, inserting her key in the door. Michael looked wonderful, she thought. He was wearing a black jacket over a white cotton shirt, and his jeans were faded and fit just right. Oh, he was beautiful, but she had the sneaky suspicion that before this conversation was concluded, Michael Patterson was going to be a bright orange. "Would you like to come in?"

"No," he said dryly, following her into the apartment and closing the door. "I just came by to hold up that wall for three hours."

"I repeat," she said, frowning up at him, "we did not have plans."

"What do I have to do? Make an appointment with your social secretary? You didn't say anything to me about being out tonight."

"You didn't ask!"

"Where in the hell were you?"

"It's none of your damn business, Patterson."

"The hell it isn't, lady! I thought about you all day, and didn't have one free minute to call. So what happens? I come charging over here to see you, and you're not even home."

"And what would you have done if I'd shown up here with a date? Rearranged his face?"

"Damn right!"

"Michael Patterson, you have a lot of nerve! Is this how you always behave when you think about a woman during the day?"

"How in the hell should I know? I never thought about a woman during the day before, Carson!"

"Well, it doesn't give you the right— You haven't?" She smiled brightly. "Never?"

"No," he said, raking his hand through his hair. "Never."

"I'll be darned," she said.

"And I didn't like it," he said, wagging a finger at her. "I have to concentrate totally on my clients. I can't have my mind wandering off on tangents about kissing and holding you. I can't be wondering what you're doing at the Honey Bee, how your day is going."

"No, of course you can't," she said sweetly. "I humbly apologize for intruding on your mental space."

"I should hope so," he said, still frowning deeply. "Don't let it happen again."

She laughed. "You *are* strung out, Mr. Patterson. I have no control over your head. Would you like a drink? Brandy?"

"Make it six," he said. He crossed the room and slouched onto the sofa.

Michael had thought about her, Mallory mused as she walked over to the liquor cabinet. Thought about kissing her, and holding her, about how her day was going. He wasn't thrilled about it, but he *had* thought about her. It had to mean something, because it had never happened to him before. So far it seemed to mean he was as happy as he might be about lower back pain. He was definitely jangled and angry. Color him red!

She carried two snifters of brandy over to the sofa and handed one to him as she sat down. He stared at the amber liquid for a long moment before he spoke.

"Well," he said, sighing, "I owe you another apology. I had no right to demand to know where you were. Damn, I can't believe I did that. Then again, I can't believe this day I've put in either." He took a large gulp of the brandy, gasped, and clutched his throat with his hand.

"That's brandy, not beer," Mallory said. "You probably dissolved your vocal cords. Actually, Michael, I don't see why you're having such a conniption simply because you thought about me on and off."

"On and off! Try all day long."

"Don't start yelling again. This isn't my fault, you know. I was minding my own business at the Honey Bee, then went out with a couple of girlfriends." And thought about you, she added silently. Constantly. But she sure as heck wasn't going to tell him that.

"Girlfriends?"

"Yes."

"Oh." He suddenly smiled. "That's nice. Have fun?"

"Yes," she said, placing her snifter on the coffee table. "But you had no right to—"

He sliced his hand through the air for silence. "Cut," he said. "I apologized because I was so off-base, it was a sin. But you have to understand, Mallory, this was a very unsettling experience for me. Maybe I've been working too hard," he added, squinting at the ceiling.

"Oh, thanks," she muttered.

"And my mother is giving me the screaming meemies. Yeah, I've overloaded my circuits."

"That was orange!" Mallory said, jumping to her feet.

"Huh?"

"I mean, rude. I am not a circuit overloader. You make me sound like one more thing on your list of nuisances. I'm a woman, not a—a pesty fly."

"Oh, darlin'," he said, grinning at her. "I know you're a woman. Believe me, Mallory, I know."

"Don't pull your good-ol'-boy routine on me, Michael."

"That's what I am. Just a laid-back, easy-goin' good ol' boy."

"Ha! You're a zoomer."

"And you," he said, grabbing her hand and pulling her down onto his lap, "are beautiful."

"Attractive," she said, her lips an inch from his.

"Beautiful," he said, his voice husky.

His tongue feathered across her lips, then he claimed her mouth in a powerful kiss that sent hot desire flooding through her entire body. She twined her arms around his neck, increasing the pressure of his mouth on hers. His tongue dueled with hers, and he crushed her against him.

Mallory relished the taste, the feel, the aroma of Michael. The colors of Michael. A flash of passion swept through her, and she trembled, causing him to tighten his hold on her.

"Mallory," he said, his voice raspy.

"Hmm?" She slowly opened her eyes.

"Remember when"—he stopped and took a steadying breath—"when I said we were doing fine?"

"Hmm? Oh, yes, I remember."

"Well, cancel that, because I for one am in deep, deep trouble here."

Five

Before Mallory could reply, Michael lifted her off his lap and deposited her on the cushion next to him. He stood and began to pace the floor, a deep frown on his face. Mallory concentrated on willing her heart to resume a normal cadence, then watched Michael as he trekked back and forth across the room.

"Strange," he muttered, as he passed her. "Very strange."

After six more trips and an assortment of incomprehensible mumblings, Mallory had had enough.

"Michael," she said, "this is all very fascinating. Or it might be if I knew what your problem was, but I don't. It's getting late and—"

"Mallory," he interrupted, halting his pacing to stand in front of her, "would you desert a man in his hour of need?"

"What?" she said, then a bubble of laughter escaped from her lips.

"Dammit, this isn't funny!"

"Michael, what are you talking about? You're babbling on and on, but I can't understand a word you're saying."

"Then I'll spell it out for you. I'm coming unglued here."

"That much is crystal-clear," she said, nodding.

"I am not accustomed to, nor will I tolerate, my thought processes being interfered with by a woman. As for my body, I'm a total wreck. I want you as I've never wanted a woman before in my life. This has got to stop. Now. This instant."

"Oh," she said, smiling. "I see."

"That's it? That's your contribution to this quandary I'm in? Thanks a lot. You and I operate on the same plane, remember? We understand the need to keep things in their proper perspective."

"You said that was regarding our work, Michael."

"Well, yeah, it is. But not entirely. What I mean is, at times it does carry over to our personal lives."

"Oh, I see."

"Quit saying that!"

"Sorry. Carry on."

"Mallory, one of the first things I learned in psychology is that people often have a deep-seated need to please their parents, and the need carries over well into the person's adult life. Due to the circumstances under which we met, there's a very good chance that's what's happening here. I'm subconsciously consumed by you out of a hidden desire to gain my mother's approval."

"That," Mallory said, flopping back on the sofa and folding her arms over her breasts, "is the most insulting thing I have ever heard. Go home, Mr. Patterson."

"No, wait," he said, sitting down next to her. "It makes sense, don't you see? Are you, yourself, behaving normally? No. You've said you're not."

"So?"

"So do you know—really know—where you're coming from? You said you were confused about your life."

"Oh, but I figured it out, and—"

"Lord, I'm brilliant," Michael rushed on. "I should send myself a bill. We're both victims of the parental-approval trap."

"You're getting insulting again. That's very close to orange, and I've had enough of this. Granted, I was muddled for a bit, but it had nothing to do with my mother. I know who I am and what I want. I got in touch with myself, and everything is perfectly clear."

"Are you sure?" he asked.

"Positive," she said, nodding decisively. "Quit lumping me into your off-the-wall syndrome. You can have it all to yourself."

"You're really squared away? You've reestablished the fact that your life is in precise order? You satisfy your maternal instincts during the day at the Honey Bee, then enter the unencumbered singles' social scene at night. Neat and tidy. No entanglements, commitments, clutter."

"Well—"

"Good for you," he interrupted again. "That's exactly where I was before I fell prey to my subconscious. The thing is, Mallory, diagnosing a problem doesn't guarantee it will automatically correct itself. We often have to meet it head-on; do battle, if you will."

"Oh?"

"Yes. Would you be willing to help me work this through? Get myself back on track?"

"How?"

"By spending time with me, a great deal of time. Overkill, my sweet. I know it's asking a lot, but it shouldn't take long. We'll operate as though we are totally committed to each other in our relationship. It will reinforce in my mind how much I don't want that type of setup, and everything will be great. The subconscious is a tricky devil, but I can beat it with your help."

Mallory studied Michael's face for a clue that he was joking, but found none. He was serious, she realized. For an intelligent man, he sure was dumb. He should be putting distance between them to accomplish his goal. Hadn't he even considered the possibility that he *wanted* to be with her?

"This is the craziest thing I've ever heard," she said, shaking her head. "You want to spend time with me so that you'll know you don't want to spend time with me?"

"Yep," he said, appearing rather pleased with himself. "Clever, huh? Will you do it? Will you help me? You wouldn't walk away from a drowning man, would you?"

"That was corny."

"I'm desperate. I pictured us having a good time

together, enjoying each other's company, but everything got out of hand."

"You pictured us going to bed together, that's what you pictured," she said, scowling at him.

"Making love. Anyway, don't worry about that part. I have my psyche to get back on the right road. I'm concentrating on the needs of my mind, not my body."

"Hooray for you," she said dryly.

"Well? Will you do it? Help me through this crisis?"

"I guess so," she said. "I still have a sneaky suspicion that I've been insulted though."

"You're a life saver," he said, gripping her by the shoulders. "Bless you."

"Now will you go home? I'm exhausted."

"You bet," he said, then gave her a quick, hard kiss. He got to his feet and strode to the door. "You're a real trouper, Mallory. See ya."

"Sure," she said wearily as the door closed behind Michael. A trooper? her mind echoed. A lunatic was closer to the mark. What a ridiculous situation. And dangerous. Michael had her pegged all wrong. She wanted everything he didn't: a permanent commitment, marriage, children. And she'd spent a good many hours today thinking about a man who wasn't remotely close to offering her what she needed. And Michael thought *he* had problems? Ha! He ought to try hers on for size.

She should be running in the opposite direction from Michael, not agreeing to spend even more time with him. And it would really help if she knew whether she had been insulted or flattered by him. It was a boost to her ego to realize she was the first woman to get him so shook up. But then again there was nothing complimentary about a man's fervent wish to rid himself of his obsession with her. Her emergence into his life was as welcome as termites, and Michael was in the process of exterminating her. What a bum. Yes, she'd definitely been insulted. But then again . . . "Oh, forget it," she said aloud. "I'm confusing myself."

Despite the turmoil in Mallory's mind her fatigue was greater, and she fell asleep within moments after crawling into bed.

The noise that intruded upon Mallory's peaceful slumber made no sense at all, and she opened one eye to peer at the clock.

"Six," she muttered. "Wonderful. Why am I awake at six in the morning? Because there's someone knocking on my door, that's why. I'll kill 'em!"

She stomped to the door, her flannel nightgown flopping against her ankles. She reached for the knob, then hesitated.

"Who is it?" she called.

"Michael."

"Michael?" she whispered. "Here? Now? Are you nuts?"

"Mallory? Open the door."

"Why not?" she said, rolling her eyes heavenward before flinging open the door.

"Hi," Michael said brightly. "How are you?"

"Dandy," she said. "What do you want?"

"Hey," he said, stepping into the apartment and shutting the door. "Is this any way to greet the man who's brought you fresh Danish? Is the coffee made?"

"No, the coffee is not made," she said, her voice rising. "It's six o'clock in the morning!"

"I wasn't sure what time you got up. You look sensational, Mallory. I love your hair when it's all tousled and wild like that. And whoever said that flannel nightgowns aren't sexy hasn't seen you in one. Gorgeous." He slid his hand around the nape of her neck. "Really beautiful," he murmured, lowering his head slowly toward her.

His mouth captured hers, his lips warm, his tongue seeking. The kiss was gentle and yet demanding, and Mallory responded instantly, feeling her breasts swell beneath the soft flannel of her nightgown. As he gathered her close to his chest she was aware of the cold fabric of his windbreaker that contrasted with her own sleepy warmth. She had the nearly uncontrollable urge to run her hands over Michael's body to drive away the chill, to kindle a raging fire. A fire that would consume her.

"Coffee," Michael said hoarsely. He slowly released her and took a step backward. "I'll fix it."

"I'll—" Mallory started, then swallowed heavily. "I'll get dressed."

"All right," he said.

But neither moved. Their eyes met and held in an endless moment. The sound of her own heartbeat echoed in Mallory's ears. Her skin was tingling, and a pulsing heat throbbed deep within her. The silence in the room was charged with sensuality that was nearly palpable in its intensity. She was aware of every rugged inch of Michael, and every part of her seemed to be begging for his kiss, his touch. She swayed slightly toward him, hardly able to breathe, aching with desire for him.

"Mallory," he said, his voice barely audible. "Go get dressed."

She blinked once slowly, dragging her mind back to reality, then turned and walked to the bedroom. She was vaguely aware that her legs felt wooden, seemingly unwilling to move her forward.

What was happening to her? she wondered frantically a few minutes later as she stood in the shower, the hot water beating against her. How long had she been pinned in place by Michael's smoldering brown gaze? What sensual power did that man hold over her? If he had kissed or touched her again, she probably would have dissolved into a heap at his feet. Had he sensed the desire within her? Had it shown in her eyes? Did he know how much she'd wanted him in that strange, timeless moment?

She was overreacting, she told herself. The entire incident had no doubt lasted only a few seconds. She was half asleep; she hadn't had her life-saving coffee. It was perfectly reasonable that things might appear distorted at six in the morning. She was under control now. Right? Wrong. Damn.

She was still unsettled as she dressed in jeans, a cable-knit red sweater, and loafers. She twisted her hair into the figure eight at the back of her head, and applied light makeup. After a deep, steadying breath, she headed for the kitchen in search of Michael.

"Coffee ready?" she asked, forcing a lightness to her voice as she entered the kitchen. "I'm really not human until I've had my coffee. I'm just a blurry blob until I've had my brew. Can't be held responsible for a thing I say or do before the first cup."

"Here you go, motor mouth," Michael said, smiling as he placed two mugs on the table.

"Thanks," she said, sliding onto a chair. "The Danish looks good. I haven't had fresh Danish in ages. Don't you have clients to see this morning? You're not exactly dressed as a spiffy lawyer."

"My first appointment isn't until ten," he said, sitting down opposite her.

"Ten? My, my, banker's hours. Well, lawyer's hours, I guess. Must be nice. I—"

"Mallory . . ."

"The Honey Bee has to open very early so that the mothers have time to get to their jobs. I don't mind, though, because—"

"Mallory."

"Would you like your Danish warmed? We could put it in the micro and—"

"Mallory!"

"Damn you, Michael," she said, resting her head on her hands. "What are you doing to me? Now I've turned into a blithering idiot. If I end up falling in love with you, I swear to heaven I'll never speak to you for as long as I live!"

Michael opened his mouth, shut it, then tried again. "What?" he said, leaning slightly toward her. "Fall in love? With me? Why would you do that? You'd mess up the game plan you have for your life."

"My life is not a game," she said, none too quietly. "I'm a woman, not a basketball player. You took courses, right? Learned how to say certain things to get a certain response from people. Yes, that's it. You're doing some kind of shrink number on me."

"I don't know what you're talking about."

"Ha! My life has been in a shambles ever since I met you when you were orange in the parking lot."

"Well, I haven't exactly been in that great shape either, lady," he said, his voice rising. "That's why I'm here, remember? I want my life back, Mallory Carson, and at the moment it's under your thumb!"

"I don't want your crummy life! Take it and shuffle off to Buffalo."

"You felt it, didn't you?" he said, his voice suddenly low and husky. "Something happened when I came in here. The air was so charged, it probably could have perked the coffee. I looked at you and— Lord, Mallory, I want you so much, I ache. You want me too. I saw it in your eyes, on your face."

"No," she said, shaking her head. "No. No. No."

"Yes, you do."

"So, yes, okay," she said, smacking the table with her hand. "I physically desire you. Satisfied? I admit it. But I'm not going to do a damn thing about it. Understand?"

"Because of this falling in love thing? I can't believe you'd allow that to happen. You said you were no longer confused about who you are, what you want."

"I'm not. Everything is very clear to me."

"Then what's the problem?"

Tell him, a voice in Mallory's head screamed. She should spell it out, tell him he was wrong about her. She wanted a husband, a lifetime commitment with a man. Michael would fall over his feet getting out the door, and she'd never see him again. Oh, dear heaven, she didn't want that. To never again be held, to be kissed by Michael Patterson. She'd miss him. And she'd be lonely.

Because. . . . She bit her lip and stared down at her coffee. Because she loved him. She'd fallen in love with Michael, she knew it, and for two cents she'd punch him right in his gorgeous nose. This was, without a doubt, the most orange thing he had ever done.

"Hey," he said, "did you die?"

She looked up at him.

"What?"

"Are you all right?"

"Yes, I'm fine." Her heart was going to be shattered into a million pieces, but other than that she was just dandy. "I told you I'm not myself before I have my coffee."

"Look," he said, taking one of her hands in his. "We're mature adults. We're both aware of the strong physical attraction we have for each other. If it were just that, we could go for it."

"Don't be crude."

"You know what I mean. We'd be wonderful together. Our lovemaking would be fabulous. It would be a glorious experience—giving, taking, sharing, discovering."

Oh-h-h, Mallory moaned inwardly. If Michael didn't shut up, she was going to faint facedown in her Danish.

"Maybe you could handle it," he went on, "but I can't, not right now. Somehow you've managed to mix up my physical with my mental, and I have to separate the two."

"You said it was Mary Louise's fault, not mine. Your ever-famous syndrome, remember?"

"Yeah, well, whatever it is, I have to correct it. You agreed to help me by spending time with me. I'm meeting this problem head-on. What you said before about falling in love—that was because you needed your caffeine fix, right?"

"Of course," she said, staring into her mug. "I'm extremely weird before my coffee. Ignore everything I said or did prior to drinking this."

"You're sure?"

"Positive," she said, sliding her hand away from his.

"Then everything is okay? You'll see me through this crisis? You understand, don't you, why I can't make love with you under these circumstances?"

"So who asked you to?" she snapped.

"*You* did," he said, his voice unbearably intimate as he looked directly into her eyes.

She was going to cry, Mallory thought frantically. She was a breath away from bursting into tears and making a complete fool of herself. Of course, falling in love with the wrong man wasn't the brightest thing she'd ever done. Oh, why didn't she just send him away, then begin the process of trying to glue herself back together? Oh, merciful heaven, not yet.

"Lord, Mallory," he said, "you look so damn sad. Is the fact that we physically desire each other that upsetting to you?"

"No. No, of course not. A lot has happened very quickly, that's all."

"No joke. We have our mothers to thank for this mess. But we'll get everything squared away, you'll see."

"Right. Well, I have to get to the Honey Bee," she said, pushing back her chair.

"I'll follow you over in my car."

"What? Why?"

"I have plenty of time to go home and change before I'm due at the office. We agreed that I should be with you as much as possible, remember? Heavy-duty commitments call for people practically living in each other's pockets. My mind is doing that already with you. I need to follow through on a physical plane to reaffirm in my brain that I want no part of being accountable to someone."

"Oh. Well, I suppose that makes sense. I can't picture you at the Honey Bee though. It's very noisy, kids running all over the place. How do you feel about grape jelly? Never mind. Do whatever you think you need to do to cure yourself of whatever it is that has you all in a dither. Lord, this is ludicrous," she said, marching from the room. "Absolutely insane."

"It is not," Michael called after her. "It's a sound, psychological plan."

"Oh, stuff it," Mallory said under her breath, as she went into the bedroom for her purse. Dumb, really dumb, she repeated silently. She was helping the man she loved rid himself of a niggling nuisance: her. So far being in love was the pits.

When she returned to the living room, he was standing by the front door. She took her jacket from the closet and slipped it on, then reached for the doorknob.

"All set," she said.

"I have to kiss you before we go."

"Why?"

"Because it's the natural thing to do before we leave our apartment to go to work. We spent the night together, then—"

"We did no such thing, Michael."

"Mentally," he said, tapping his temple with his finger, "I spent the night with you."

"No kidding?" she said, an instant smile on her face. "What did we do?"

"Don't ask."

"It was that good, huh?" she said, wiggling her eyebrows up and down.

"Knock it off."

"Sorry. Okay, so now you kiss me. Make it fast, I don't want to be late."

"That was cold!"

"Look, you're the one taking the cure or whatever. I'm trying to cooperate, but it's rather unsettling to feel like an actress playing out a part. Don't expect me to get excited about a kiss you penned into the script. Talk about clinical. Geez."

"There is nothing clinical about my kisses, Mallory Carson!"

"Would you quit analyzing it to death and just do it?"

"All right," he growled, and hauled her into his arms.

His mouth came down hard onto hers, and Mallory was instantly lost. This kiss was not cold and clinical. Oh, no. It was the familiar, wonderful color of fire. Hot, burning flames of desire were licking throughout her. Oh, the taste of Michael, the feel of his lips and tongue. Ecstasy. And, oh Lord, how she loved him.

He slowly lifted his head, his breathing unsteady as he trailed his thumb over her cheek.

"Erase clinical," she said.

"I should hope so. But you had a valid point. From now on I won't kiss you just because it fits the program. All kisses will be . . . kisses. Real, separate and apart from the problem at hand. Got that? There will be nothing phony about my holding you, kissing you."

"That's nice," she said dreamily.

"Yeah." He started leaning toward her, then snapped his head back up. "Time to go," he said. "The Honey Bee awaits."

"I won't fire myself if I'm late. The other women are always on time."

"Bad plan." He opened the door. "Out. Go."

"Don't you want to kiss me again?"

He groaned. "Mallory, please. Just go, will ya?"

"It's a perfectly reasonable question, Michael."

"Mallory!"

"All right!"

The morning air was chilly, and Mallory hurried across the parking lot to her car as Michael headed for his. She waited until he was behind her before pulling out into the traffic.

The sports car suited him, she decided, glancing often in the rearview mirror. It was sleek and powerful, and a person would have to be an expert to understand all of its complexities. The same description applied to Michael. Oh, what was she going to do? She didn't have the strength to send him away, but he was going to leave her eventually. As soon as he worked through his mental dilemma, he would walk out of her life.

And in the meantime? she asked herself. She'd hang on to Michael Patterson for dear life for as long as he was there. Lord, where was her pride? Mallory Carson in love was a new and startling creature. Borderline nauseating too. Imagine clinging to each day with Michael like an hysterical female. No, like a woman in love, and there were no set rules here. And what about the nights? As she filled her heart and mind with memories of Michael, would they include the lovemaking they had shared?

Yes. She was absolutely, positively going to make love with Michael Patterson. Although, that could be rather tough to do considering Michael had no intention of making love with her. He was separating his mental self from his physical self, or some such thing. Well, hell's bells, she had rights too. So far she was doing everything by Michael's rules. Well, no more Mr. Nice Guy. She wanted that man's body! Oh, good grief. Shame on her. She was starting to sound like her mother.

But was it fair, Mallory wondered, to seduce Michael—providing, of course, that she could— when he felt he wasn't mentally prepared to handle their making love? Oh, dear, now her conscience was sticking its nose in her business. She was definitely going to have to think this through. Darn.

With a sigh Mallory turned into the parking lot at the Honey Bee. Michael whipped into the space next to her and they met at the front of her car.

"Nice building," he said, his gaze sweeping over the structure.

"I had it specially designed to accommodate the childrens' needs. Come inside and— Oh, Lord, why are you here?"

"What?"

"My friend Patty, who works here, knows you're Mary Louise's son. If the mothers catch wind of the fact that you came here, they'll blow it all out of proportion."

"Good point. Okay, I'm here to broaden the scope of my psychological studies so I can further incorporate them into my law practice. I'll be observing the children of divorced parents, their social adjustments, how they relate to other children and adults. How's that?"

"Brilliant," she said, smiling up at him. "You're good at what you do, aren't you?"

"Yes, I am," he said quietly. "I'm good because the people who come to me deserve to have the best available help. Sound conceited as hell?"

"It sounds wonderful," she said. And she loved him even more for it. How would she bear it when this man walked out of her life? He had stroked once silent chords within her, and now her whole being seemed to sing with joy when she was with him. Lord, how she loved him.

"Do I get the tour now?" Michael asked, bringing her from her reverie.

"Yes, of course, come inside. I'm a bit late after all, so you'll be greeted by the pitter-patter of little feet."

Inside she showed Michael the various rooms and introduced him to the staff. Patty beamed and shook his hand.

"So, you're Mikey . . . I mean, Michael Patterson," she said. "Your mother is a doll."

"She can also be a holy terror when she puts her mind to it," he said, smiling. "But she says that about me, too, so it comes out even."

"Well, my Andy adores her. He doesn't have a grandmother, and he thoroughly enjoys both Mary Louise and Clarissa. Oh, Mallory, Amy's mother said that Amy's father will be picking her up here tonight for the weekend. I had her sign the release saying it was all right to allow him to do that. Amy is upset, and she said she's not going to her daddy's house anymore. I tried to talk to her, but she's very sullen."

"I'll speak with her," Mallory said. "Poor little thing. She just hasn't adjusted to the upheavals in her life."

"Is she the one you told me about in the restaurant that day?" Michael asked.

Mallory looked up at him in surprise. "Yes. I'm amazed you remembered."

"Father remarried after the divorce?"

"Yes."

"Would you like me to chat with her a bit?"

"You wouldn't mind?" Mallory said. "I've run out of things to say to her, and her mother is terribly concerned."

"Well, I'll just ask her what she's up to, how she's feeling, see if I can pick up on anything. Where is she?"

"Over there by the window in the pink corduroy dress."

He nodded and crossed the room to a window about three feet away from Amy, then stood there, staring outside.

"What is he doing?" Patty whispered to Mallory.

"I don't know," Mallory said.

"Mallory, that is the most gorgeous, most sexy, most manly man these tired old eyes have ever feasted upon."

"Yes, he's . . . handsome."

"Handsome? He's a knockout! He's dripping with charisma, with—"

"Patty, hush, he'll hear you. Look, he's pointing out the window. From the way she's shaking her head, I gather Amy didn't like what he said."

They watched as Michael crouched down to eye level with the little girl. "Oh," Patty sighed. "Look at those thighs beneath those faded jeans."

"Patty!"

"Mallory Carson, don't be so stuffy. I can gawk if I want to. I give you permission to get miffed at me only if I start drooling on his shirt front."

"Oh, okay," Mallory said, laughing. "I'll keep that in mind. Look at them."

Michael had turned to sit on the carpeted floor, his back against the wall, legs crossed at the ankle. Amy was next to him in the exact same pose. They were in the process of measuring the size of her hand against his. Then they compared the length of their feet. Finally Michael covered his heart with his hand and continued to talk to Amy, who was gazing up at him with wide eyes.

"I understand," Mallory whispered. "Or I think I do. He's telling her that daddies have bigger hands and feet than little girls. Now, he's talking about the love in daddies' hearts. I'm sure of it, Patty. He's saying her father has a big enough heart to love her *and* his new family."

"Oh, good grief," Patty said. "I'm going to cry."

And she was going to love, Mallory thought. Forever.

More children arrived in a steady stream over the next fifteen minutes, and Mallory greeted each one while acutely aware that Michael and Amy kept talking. When Michael finally began to stand, Mallory's throat tightened with emotion as Amy threw her arms around his neck. He held her close for a long moment, then tickled her into a giggling bundle before he walked slowly back to Mallory.

"Neat kid," he said.

"Thank you," she said, blinking back her tears. "You were talking about how much love her father has in his heart, weren't you?"

"We worked up to that," he said, nodding. "I

insulted the color of your swing sets first, then moved on to the good stuff. She's confused, Mallory, and feels displaced. Her father needs to reassure her she's just as important and loved as she always was."

"I'll speak with him when he picks her up today. I can't thank you enough, Michael."

"I'll ditto that," Patty said as she breezed by. "By the way, the Marines have landed."

"Hold it," Mallory said. "What are you talking about?"

"Mary Louise and Clarissa just came in the front door."

Six

"Oh, good Lord," Mallory said, looking frantically at Michael.

"Don't panic," he said. "The same story holds. I'm here doing research. Come on, we'll meet the dynamic duo in the hall."

"But . . ." Mallory started, then hurried to keep up with Michael's long-legged stride.

In the hallway Michael stopped so abruptly that Mallory bumped into him. Clarissa and Mary Louise were still by the front door, hanging up their coats on a wooden rack.

"Just stay cool," Michael said out of the corner of his mouth. "Don't blow this caper now, sweetheart."

"You still do a lousy Bogart," Mallory said. "Would you listen to me for a minute? *I* was the one who told you about the Honey Bee that day at the restaurant. You would have had to have seen me since the night at the police station to even know this place existed."

"Oh, good Lord, to use your phrase," Michael said. "Is there a back door to this building?"

"What happened to staying cool, sweetheart?" she asked.

"The jig is up. We've blown our cover."

"Michael, stop it. The mothers mustn't think there's anything going on between us."

"I'll come up with something," he said. "I hope."

Clarissa and Mary Louise turned and started down the hall. They smiled brightly the instant they spotted the pair waiting for them. Mallory groaned silently.

"Mikey," Mary Louise said, beaming up at him, "what a surprise."

"It's Michael," he said. "Hello, Mother, Clarissa."

"It's marvelous seeing you again, Michael," Clarissa said. "Good morning, Mallory dear."

"Hi," she said weakly.

"What are you doing here, Mikey?" Mary Louise asked.

"Michael. I'm here in a professional capacity to observe the social and antisocial adjustments, or lack of same, of the child of divorced parents. Said subjects are being raised in an environment different from past generations, and it's imperative that an evaluation be done of their maturity level, charted on a standard bell curve, so we might project their impact on society at large at a later date."

"That's right," Mallory said, her head bobbing up and down. "Isn't that fascinating?" She hadn't understood all of what Michael had said, she thought, trying desperately not to laugh. What a spiel.

"What's fascinating," Mary Louise said, "is that you chose the Honey Bee to conduct your study. I don't recall ever mentioning that Mallory owned this day-care center."

"You don't?" Michael said, raising his eyebrows. "You don't remember telling me about the Honey Bee? Well, don't be alarmed, Mother. It's not unusual to forget little details at your age."

"Michael Francis Patterson, I do not forget little details," Mary Louise said indignantly.

"Francis?" Mallory repeated in a burst of laughter. "Francis?" Michael shot her a stormy look.

"Just how *did* you know about the Honey Bee, Michael?" Clarissa asked.

"How did I know about the Honey Bee," he said. "Yes. Well. I knew about the Honey Bee because . . . because . . ." He threw his arm around Mallory's shoulders and hauled her to his side. "Mallory and I have no secrets between us. Since the moment we met in the romantic atmosphere of the police-station parking lot, we've been inseparable. We've laughed, talked, shared . . . and stuff. We are on the brink of discovery."

"Do you have a screw loose?" Mallory shrieked, trying to wiggle out of Michael's embrace. He tightened his hold.

"She's shy," he said. "Isn't that cute? Now, now, darling, there's nothing to be embarrassed about."

"You're a dead man, Patterson," she said through clenched teeth.

"Oh-h-h, this is wonderful," Mary Louise said, clasping her hands. "I'm so thrilled, I could weep with joy."

"Oh, my," Clarissa said, pressing her hands to her cheeks. "This is splendid, splendid. I told Mallory that you certainly knew how to fill out a pair of—"

"Mother!" Mallory yelled.

"Well, he does," Clarissa said, lifting her chin naughtily. "He's a very sexy man."

"Thank you," Michael said solemnly. "You've made my day, Clarissa."

"I don't believe this," Mallory said, rolling her eyes to the heavens. "This is a nightmare, and I'm going to wake up."

"You're so adorable," Michael said, kissing her on the temple. Clarissa and Mary Louise sighed wistfully. Mallory groaned. "Now, then," Michael went on, "here's the plan. The four of us are going to my cabin on Mount Lemmon for the weekend."

"What?" Mallory whispered.

"Why?" Clarissa asked, frowning. "Wouldn't you rather be alone with Mallory? How are you going to discover what you're on the brink of discovering with a couple of old ladies tagging along?"

"Chaperons you do not need," Mary Louise said, poking Michael in the chest with her finger. "Are you, or are you not, your father's son?"

"I assume I am," Michael said. "Unless you had something going with the mailman way back when that you'd like to confess."

"You know what I mean," Mary Louise said, whopping him on the arm.

"I want to go home," Mallory muttered, but no one paid any attention to her.

"Listen up," Michael said. "I'm the one with a degree in psychology, remember? I know exactly what I'm doing. Mallory and I are extremely family-oriented people. In other words we feel a fierce loyalty to you two. It is imperative to our mental well-being that we are assured that the four of us can function as a unit so that there is no undue strain on our relationship. We realize that the two of you are best friends, but meshing families is another ball game. We can't proceed with our discovering, per se, until we know that there is harmony within the ranks. Hence the trip to the cabin."

"I'm going to throw up," Mallory mumbled.

"Oh," Clarissa said, appearing rather confused.

"Could you run that by me again?" Mary Louise asked.

"No time," Michael said. "I have clients to see. Will you excuse us, ladies? I'd like to say good-bye to Mallory privately." He began to move toward the office with Mallory in tow. "I'll pick you two up around eight tomorrow morning to go to the Lemon. Pack warm clothes. It'll be nippy up there. Bye." He propelled Mallory into her office and closed the door behind them.

Mallory immediately stepped away from Michael, planted her hands on her hips, and glared at him. He raised his hands in a gesture of peace, and backed up until he thudded against the wall.

"Now, don't get excited," he said. "I can explain everything."

She slowly advanced toward him, her hands in tight fists at her sides, blue eyes flashing with anger.

"I'm going to strangle you with my bare hands," she said. "I'm going to toss you off the top of the

Transamerica building. I'm going to feed you to the polar bears at the Reid Park Zoo."

"There's a streak of supressed violence in you, do you know that?" he said. "I can explain."

"Speak, Patterson. You have three seconds."

"Look, it was a very touchy situation. Our mothers are sharp as tacks. If I'd said we'd had lunch the day after the jailbird bit, they might have figured out we'd been discussing them as though they were naughty children. That would have demolished them, Mallory; blown their self-esteem straight to hell. I couldn't run that risk."

"Go on," she said, staring hard at him.

"The weekend will serve a double purpose. You and I will be together, as we agreed. We'll go for walks in the woods, stuff like that. But while in the company of the mothers, we'll squabble."

"What? Why?"

"To nip in the bud any matchingmaking scheme they've cooked up. Right now, they're thrilled that we're together, but they'll come to see that we're incompatible. They wouldn't want us to be unhappy. They'll be all in favor of us going our separate ways."

"I see," Mallory said quietly. "And that, of course, is your ultimate goal too. You want to be free of whatever this strange hold is I have on you. Well, all right, Michael, I'll cooperate fully with your plans for the weekend."

"Great," he said, smiling. "You're a real—"

"Trouper. Yes, I know." She would *not* cry, she told herself. But, oh, it hurt, all of it. She loved Michael so much, and he wanted nothing more than to be free of her. He'd even concocted a way to assure that their mothers wouldn't be pushing her at him in the future. No, she mustn't cry, because once she started she might never be able to stop. "Well," she said, "you'd better get going or you'll be late for your first appointment."

"Right." He closed the distance between them and circled her waist with his arms. "Is something wrong?"

"No, of course not. It's just been a rather hectic morning. I want to thank you again for talking to Amy."

"Like I said, she's a neat kid. She informed me that the bow in her hair matched her dress perfectly. I liked that. In spite of her fears she still felt good about herself to a certain degree. There was a man, a client of mine, who had lost his legs in an accident. His wife couldn't handle it and served him with divorce papers. Well, the guy was a wreck. Every time we met and started to talk things through, he cried. He'd pull out a pristine, freshly ironed handkerchief and cry. I finally asked him about those handkerchiefs. He said, 'I may blubber like a baby but, by God, I'll do it with class.' At that moment I knew he was going to make it, and he did."

"Oh, Michael," Mallory said, a sob catching in her throat.

"Hey, I'm sorry. I didn't mean to upset you."

"No, you didn't. I just . . . Michael, please kiss me. I realize I'm acting strangely, but ignore it and kiss me. Please."

His mouth captured her sob as his lips melted over hers. It was a gentle kiss, as though he were suddenly afraid she'd shatter like fragile china.

She twined her hands behind his neck and forced his lips harder onto hers, thrusting her tongue deep into his mouth. He groaned, and a shudder of response swept through him. The kiss became urgent, frenzied, as an unnoticed tear slid down Mallory's cheek.

Michael pulled her tightly to him, her breasts crushing against his chest. She relished the sweet pain, and the rough onslaught of Michael's mouth on hers. She wanted only to feel him, to taste him. She wanted to be consumed by sensations, not by thoughts, truths, facts about her hopeless situation. She wanted his body to speak of his need of her, for he would never utter the words of love. She clung to him as if she'd never let him go again.

"No more," he said finally, his voice raspy with passion.

"I'm sorry," she said, as she took a step backward.

"Oh, Mallory." He trailed his thumb over the tear track on her cheek. "What's wrong? Did I hurt you? I didn't mean to be so rough."

"No, no, you didn't hurt me. It's just been an emotionally draining morning. I'm fine, really I am. You've got to leave or you're going to be terribly late."

He frowned as he studied her pale face. "Are you sure you're all right?" he asked.

"Positive," she said, managing a weak smile.

"How's this? I'll give the mothers some money and put them in charge of getting the food for the cabin. Then you won't have to put up with them being here all day badgering you with questions about us."

"Yes, fine."

"I'll talk to you later," he said, then brushed his lips over hers. "Bye."

"Good-bye," she said softly.

After Michael had closed the door behind him, Mallory crossed the room and sank wearily into her chair. She rested her elbows on the top of the desk and massaged her aching temples. The events of the morning, from the moment Michael had arrived at her apartment, tumbled together in her mind.

A lifetime in just hours, she mused. That was what it seemed like. She had gained so much insight into who Michael was as a man, a lawyer, a son. He was even more sensitive and caring than she had imagined. Yes, a lifetime. That was how long she felt she had known him—and loved him. Michael had all the qualities she had ever hoped to find in a man—except one. He didn't love her, didn't believe in love and committing himself to a woman. She was so close, yet so very far from obtaining the happiness she had dreamed about. It was hopeless, and that realization brought an ache to her heart and fresh tears to her eyes.

With a wobbly sigh Mallory stood and walked into the small bathroom off her office. After splashing cold water on her face, she squared her shoulders, lifted her chin, and plastered a smile on her face. A knock sounded at the office door.

"Come in," she called.

Clarissa opened the door and poked her head inside. "We're off to the market," she said. "Mary Louise and I are in charge of grub. That's cabin jargon for food."

"Oh, I see," Mallory said, laughing. "Well, I'm sure you'll assemble some delicious grub."

"Mallory," Clarissa said, coming into the office, "you're awfully pale. Aren't you feeling well?"

"I feel just fine. I must have forgotten to dust some blusher on my cheeks this morning."

"Well, that's understandable. You definitely have other things on your mind. What a shock—a wonderful one, of course—to see you and Michael together. Oh, Mallory, he's a marvelous young man, and he obviously cares for you. You're such a handsome couple. I just wish, well . . ."

"Wish what, Mother?"

"You're my daughter, dear. I realize you're a grown woman, but that doesn't diminish my motherly instincts. I just sense that something isn't quite right. I saw you with Michael, I heard the things he said, but there's an aura of tension around you, dear. Michael appeared relaxed and happy. But are you happy, Mallory?"

No, Mallory screamed silently. Her heart was splintering into a million pieces. She was going to cry for the next decade. That did not add up to happy. "Yes, of course, I am," she said. "Everything has happened very quickly, that's all. Now, you go off on your mission for grub, and don't worry about me. We're all going to have a fantastic weekend on Mount Lemmon. Maybe it will snow up there. Wouldn't that be fun? I hope I can remember where I put my mittens. I've got to go help Patty. She'll think I've deserted her."

"You're talking too fast," Clarissa said, frowning. "That's a definite sign that you're—"

"Excited," Mallory said. She scooted around her

mother and headed for the door. "Who wouldn't be? I have an extraordinary new man in my life, a nifty weekend to look forward to, all kinds of great stuff. I'll see you in the morning, Mother. Ta-ta."

"Ta-ta, dear," Clarissa said, still frowning.

The morning was hectic, and Mallory was grateful for the ongoing demands of the children. That way she had little time to dwell on the hopelessness of her relationship with Michael. After lunch the children rested, and Mallory stood by Amy's cot, watching the little girl sleep. Her gaze fell on the pink bow in Amy's hair, and she smiled as she realized that it did, indeed, perfectly match the corduroy dress.

Michael's words skittered through her mind, and she recalled the importance he had placed on Amy's pride in her special ribbon. And then she thought of the man with his carefully ironed handkerchiefs. He would cry with class, he had said.

A pink satin ribbon, Mallory pondered, walking slowly down the hall. Her self-esteem. Darn it, was she, or was she not, the first woman to throw Mr. Michael Patterson into a tailspin? Yes, she was.

"Well, hooray for me," she said aloud, a sudden smile on her face. "I didn't know I had it in me."

Self-esteem, she thought. She had upset Michael's peaceful existence by doing nothing more than lazily being herself. Talk about self-esteem. What if she got serious about this? Launched a campaign to capture the elusive heart of Michael Patterson—confirmed bachelor extraordinaire?

But what if she failed? She would still cry if she lost Michael, but at least this way she'd know she'd been every inch a woman as she'd fought for the love of her man. Yes, she'd still cry, but she'd cry with class!

Mallory never stopped smiling the rest of the day. Her depression had vanished into thin air, and she felt alive, tingling with excitement. When Amy's father arrived at the Honey Bee, Mallory asked him to step into her office, where she explained what had transpired between Amy and Michael. The man was so grateful to have some clue to his daughter's obvious unhappiness, he shook Mallory's hand until she was convinced it was going to fall off. She knew Amy's father had listened to every word she'd said when she heard him tell his daughter how impressed he was that her hair ribbon matched her dress. Amy beamed.

"Thank you, Michael," Mallory whispered as she watched father and daughter leave the Honey Bee hand in hand.

The Friday-night traffic was heavy as Mallory drove home, and it took her nearly twice as long as usual to get home. The telephone was ringing as she entered her apartment.

"Hello?" she said breathlessly, after snatching up the receiver.

"You're late," a deep voice said.

"Michael?"

"It better be," he said gruffly. "Who else knows exactly when you're due home?"

She frowned. "You're in a good mood. What is your problem, sir?"

"Damn it, Mallory, I was worried about you. Do you know what the statistics are for having an automobile accident within a ten-mile radius of your own home?"

"No, I don't," she said, smiling. "What are the statistics for having an accident between here and there?"

"Oh. Well, I don't actually know, but I'm sure they're grim."

"Well, it was very nice of you to be concerned, but I'm safe and sound right here in my living room." He cared about her! her heart sang. He did, he did, he did. "Where are you?" she asked.

"Still at my office, and I will be for hours. Due to the fact that a certain young woman has scrambled my brain circuits, I completely forgot I'm leaving for California Monday morning to attend a conference. Since I'm the keynote speaker, the appropriate thing would be to write a speech for the damn thing."

"How long will you be gone?"

"I'll be back late Wednesday night."

"Oh."

"Well, I'd better get started on this speech. I really would like to see you tonight, but I guess I'll have to settle for early tomorrow morning. Do you . . . uh, are you staying home this evening?"

"Well, let me see," Mallory said slowly. "Yes, I believe I am. I'm in the mood for a long bubble bath."

"Bubble bath? With bubbles?"

"Lots of bubbles, honeysuckle-scented bubbles. I'll put some dreamy music on the stereo, turn off all the lights, and burn a candle in the bathroom. All that together creates an unbe-e-elievable atmosphere."

"Lord," Michael moaned. "I'm dying."

"I adore the way my skin feels after a bubble bath, all silky and smooth and—"

"Mallory!"

"Yes, Michael?" she said, pure innocence ringing in her voice.

"Nothing. Enjoy your bath. See you in the morning. Bye."

"Ta-ta," she said breezily, then hung up the receiver. "Gotcha, Patterson," she said, laughing. "I gotcha good."

As she started toward the kitchen with thoughts of food, the telephone rang again. She spun around and answered it cheerfully.

"Damn it, Mallory!" Michael roared.

"Oh, good Lord," she said, covering her heart with her hand. "You scared me to death."

"That will save me the trouble of wringing your neck! How am I supposed to concentrate on a speech about incorporating psychology into law practices specializing in divorce, when I'm picturing you in a bubble bath complete with candlelight and soft music? Tell me, Mallory, how am I supposed to do that?"

"Well, my goodness," she said, suppressing her laughter. "Did I disrupt your train of thought? I do apologize. I was merely chatting about how I planned to spend my evening. Here. Alone. With the door locked against the noise and confusion of the world. Ah, so peaceful, tranquil, and so many bubbles."

"Mallory, I'm warning you, knock it off."

"You certainly are crabby, Michael."

"Because you're driving me nuts!"

"Tsk, tsk."

"That's all. I've had it. I'm hanging up now and writing my speech. I refuse to give one more moment's thought to you and your damnable bubbles. Understand? I am taking back control of my mind, Mallory."

"Of course, you are, Michael," she said ever so sweetly. "Just push me from your mind and write your cute little speech. I'm sure it will be brilliant. Oh, by the way, which do you think would have the nicer fragrance, honeysuckle bubbles or lilac?"

He groaned. "I can't stand it."

"See you in the morning," Mallory said.

"Yeah," he said, then hung up with a less than gentle touch.

Mallory was smiling as she slowly replaced the receiver, then trailed her fingers along the white plastic. The image of Michael, the very essence of Michael, washed over her, and desire tingled throughout her body. She closed her eyes to savor each sensation that was now sweeping through her. It was as though Michael were there, close, about to reach out and—

"Good Lord," she said, her eyes popping open as she felt her passion rising. "Go eat dinner, Mallory Carson."

There was no way, Mallory decided an hour later, that she was going to create the seductive bathtub scene she had dangled under Michael's nose. She couldn't handle it. If she had been consumed by the thought of him while eating an overcooked hamburger, she'd never survive the bubble bit.

She missed Michael, she knew it, and refused to allow the realization to upset her. It was too late to hold back any of her feelings. She loved him, pure and simple. She was half of a whole, part of a pair. The other member of the duo wasn't exactly cooperating, but she was working on that.

Darn it, she thought, as she pulled her hand-tooled leather overnight bag from the closet, didn't Michael see the significance of his concern when she'd been late arriving home? Didn't he realize that he genuinely cared for her? Weren't people with bachelor's degrees in psychology supposed to be smarter than that? No, maybe not. He was a man first, a psychologist second. A man who had never been in love and probably wouldn't recognize the emotion if it hit him in the head.

The really lousy part was, she decided, that Michael was struggling for all he was worth to rid himself of his obsession with her. Now, *that* was extremely orange behavior. Well, Mr. Patterson had better gear up, because she was ready to do battle. She was fighting for his love. She was fighting for her life.

By seven-thirty the next morning Mallory was a nervous wreck. She had spent a restless night tossing and turning, dozing occasionally, only to dream of Michael. The trip to Mount Lemmon was holding less and less appeal. She did *not* want to stage phony arguments with Michael to convince their mothers that the lovebirds were not meant for each other. She wanted to make love, not war!

She plucked a thread from her kelly-green sweater, then ran her moist palms over her jean-clad legs. Her hair was a shiny dark cloud that tumbled past her shoulders, her makeup light but expertly applied. She was as ready as she'd ever be, she supposed, but she didn't want to go. What if the weekend on the Lemon was all Michael needed to accomplish his damnable cure?

A knock sounded at the door and she moved to answer it, her thoughts bleak. She forced a smile onto her face and opened the door.

"Hi," Michael said.

"Hello. Come in." She stepped back for him to enter, then closed the door after him.

"Oh, Mallory," he said, weaving his fingers through the silken cascade of her hair. "You look beautiful. I love your hair like this."

And *she* loved *him*, Mallory thought. Pride, self-esteem, pink satin ribbons. She had to carry on!

"Really beautiful," he said, his voice low and husky. He cradled her face in his hands and lowered his head.

A tiny gasp of pleasure escaped from Mallory as his mouth covered hers. He took advantage and slipped his tongue past her parted lips and into the inner darkness of her mouth. She responded totally, the desire that remained a glowing ember within her bursting instantly into a raging fire. She felt hot. Burning. The moan deep in her throat was matched by Michael's. His kiss stole the breath from her body, and left her aching with her need for him.

"Oh, Mallory," he said hoarsely as he slowly lifted his head. "There ought to be a law against what you do to me."

She blinked once, then twice, but made no attempt to speak as she gazed up at him.

"Don't look at me like that," he said, stepping back. "I *know* there's a law against where my mind is going at the moment."

"There's a law against making love?" she asked, amazed she had a voice.

"Well, no, but making love is a jointly agreed upon decision and— Enough. I can't handle any more of this conversation. Where's your suitcase?" he asked, glancing around the room. "Are you ready to go?"

"Yes," she said softly. "I'm ready, Michael."

His head snapped around, and he frowned slightly as he studied her face. She lifted her chin and met his gaze steadily.

He had picked up on her innuendo, she thought. She knew he had. He was mulling it over, and appeared as though he were struggling within himself. She had said it. She had let him know she was ready to make love with him. What was he thinking? What would he do? What would he say?

"Let's go," he said gruffly, averting his eyes from hers. "Our mothers are waiting. Mary Louise stayed overnight at Clarissa's, so we have only one stop to make."

"All right," Mallory said, sighing. So much for that, she thought sadly. If she was so beautiful, why wasn't she irresistible? Darn. When Michael made up his mind about something, he was a very stubborn son of a gun. This was going to be even tougher than she'd anticipated.

Outside in the parking lot Mallory suddenly stopped.

"Wait a minute," she said. "How can four people fit in a sports car that holds two?"

"They don't. I have a Bronco with four-wheel drive. This way, madam," he said, with a sweep of his arm.

"I'm impressed, sir," she said, smiling. "And

what, pray tell, is this cabin like that we're all cramming ourselves into?"

"Not bad. I figure that in another year I'll have enough money to get electricity and indoor plumbing."

"What?" she said, her eyes widening. "You mean, there's no— Oh, good Lord."

"What a shame," Michael said, shaking his head. "You won't be able to take one of those bubble baths of yours."

"Wonderful," she mumbled. Michael laughed.

Clarissa and Mary Louise were watching out the window when Michael drove up, and the two small boxes of food were soon loaded into the vehicle. The mothers chattered on about various topics as Michael drove toward the Santa Catalina Mountains on the edge of town. The top of majestic Mount Lemmon was hidden by heavy, low-hanging clouds, and Michael remarked that the skiers were no doubt hoping for snow.

Mallory had been to Mount Lemmon many times, and was not overly fond of the twisting road that snaked its way steeply upward. Michael handled the Bronco with expertise, taking the curves with maximum care. Mallory began to relax, until she thought of an outhouse, a cold outhouse, inhabited by creepy, crawling creatures.

"Yuck," she said.

"What?" Michael asked.

"Nothing. Mother, did you bring your camera to take pictures for your book?"

"We've chucked the book," Clarissa said. "We have twenty-four pictures of Mary Louise's index finger because she had it over the lens. My roll of film was blank, totally blank. Don't ask me how that happened."

"The book is a washout, huh?" Michael said. "My sympathies, ladies."

"It's not that important," Clarissa said, shrugging. "On to more challenging endeavors. Right, Mary Louise?"

"Oh, absolutely," Mary Louise said. "I know our editor will be disappointed, but that's the breaks. He'll get over it."

Mallory and Michael exchanged smiles.

"Another ten minutes," Michael said finally. "Hey, it's starting to snow. It's going to be like a fairy-land up here. Gorgeous."

Very, *very* cold outhouse, Mallory thought, wrinkling her nose. Whose stupid idea was this? Well, maybe all the creepy, crawling creatures would freeze to death.

"Mikey dear," Mary Louise said, "Clarissa and I have had a slight change of plans."

"It's Michael. What kind of change of plans?"

"Well, I know you wanted us all to be together up here, but we can do that down in town. There's a bridge marathon being held at the lodge, and Clarissa and I called and had places reserved for us at the tables."

"What?" Mallory and Michael said in unison.

"Just drive us directly to the lodge," Mary Louise went on. "You know how I love bridge, Mikey. You wouldn't want me to give up the chance to be in a marathon, would you?"

"No. No, of course not," he said, frowning. "You just took me by surprise. I hope you and Clarissa have a great time."

"You can pick us up tomorrow whenever you're ready to go back home," Mary Louise said.

"Yeah, right," Michael said, still frowning.

Several voices were screaming in Mallory's mind. No mothers? No chaperons? She and Michael were going to be alone overnight in that cabin? *Alone?* She had to calm down, to think this through. It was actually the perfect turn of events. She wanted to have Michael all to herself, to give him no choice but to concentrate only on her and hopefully realize how much he sincerely cared for her. And she wanted to make love with him. Whatever the ultimate outcome of their relationship was, she wanted to have shared that special union with the only man she had ever loved. So, okay, fine. They'd be alone. Oh, help!

She stole a glance at Michael from the corner of her eye and saw that his grip on the steering wheel had tightened to the point that his knuckles had turned white. Despite his calm words to his mother, Michael was not thrilled with the change of plans. Well, Mallory thought, thanks a whole helluva lot. Not everyone got a chance to have her fabulous body all to himself in an isolated cabin. The man should be counting his blessings.

"Well," he said, "there's the lodge. We'll drop you two cardsharps off, then Mallory and I will head for the cabin."

Alone, Mallory's mind echoed. Alone.

Seven

Clarissa and Mary Louise disappeared into the lodge, still chattering a blue streak. Michael turned the Bronco around and started back down the road.

"I'll bet ten bucks," he said, "that there's no bridge marathon. Erase what I said about staying a step ahead of those two."

"They mean well," Mallory said quietly.

"So much for that great plan."

"Well, I'm just as glad we don't have to pretend to argue, Michael. I'm not as actress and, besides, it seemed rather dishonest."

"Desperate men do desperate things. Are you ready for this one? After I managed to quit imagining you in that damn bubble bath of yours and concentrate on my speech, I started thinking about Amy. You know, wondering how she was getting along with her father, whether or not he'd been receptive to what you said to him."

"That's very thoughtful of you," Mallory said, staring out the side window.

Michael smacked the steering wheel with his palm, causing Mallory to jump in her seat.

"Thoughtful?" he said. "No, it's a man out of control. Do you know why I was thinking of Amy? Because she's connected with you, and it upsets you when she's unhappy. Yes, I want Amy and her family to get all squared away, but my main concern is for you, Mallory."

"And you really hate that, don't you?" she said, shifting in her seat to face him. "You can't stand it that you're concerned about me when I get home late, or when I'm trying to help a little girl. Damn it, Michael." Her voice started to rise. "Do you resent me so much that you're angry over a few caring thoughts? Are you that wrapped up in yourself?" Oh, good Lord, she thought instantly. What a rotten thing to say. She knew how much Michael cared for other people—and her. The issue was that he didn't like being out of control about that caring.

He jerked his head around to look at her, then immediately redirected his attention to the road, his jaw tightly clenched.

"Wrapped up in myself?" he repeated in a low voice. "Self-centered? Selfish? Is that how you see me? I thought you understood where I was coming from. I give myself to my clients all day under very emotionally draining circumstances. My personal life is mine, and I have to protect it because it's all I have left. If I start slicing up that pie, too, what happens to me, the man?"

"I know," Mallory said, sighing. "I'm sorry. I understand what you're saying."

"And you conduct your life the same way."

"No, I—"

"Here's the cabin," he said, turning into a narrow driveway.

Mallory's gaze swept over the brick structure. "Cabin," she said. "That's a house, a real house. You rat." She punched him on the arm. "You wouldn't believe the gruesome image I had in my mind."

He laughed. "A little building in the back with a half moon on the door?"

"Complete with creepy, crawling creatures. You're a bum."

He turned off the ignition. "I bought this place from some people who used to live here year-round. They were getting old and decided the drive was becoming too much for them, so they moved back down to town. Come on, I'll give you the tour."

"I'll carry a box of food. I mean grub."

"I'll bring it in later," he said, opening the door. "I want to get the heat turned on inside, and a fire going."

"Well, no sense in wasting a trip. I'll get that box with the—"

"No," he said firmly. "You don't have to tote heavy things. That's my job, and I'm here to do it. Let's go."

"Whatever," she said, opening her door and sliding off the seat. How macho and chauvinistic could a person get? she wondered. He'd practically said, "Me Tarzan, you Jane." And it was the dearest, sweetest thing she'd ever heard. However, if Mr. Patterson thought she was doing all the cooking because it was woman's work, he had another think coming.

The snow was falling heavier in big, wet flakes, and she tilted her head back and stuck out her tongue to catch a snowflake. She laughed in delight, then noticed Michael was staring at her.

"You looked like a little girl when you did that," he said.

She smiled. "I couldn't resist. I don't see snow very often."

"It's on your hair, like drops of crystal, or lacy dew. You're so damn beautiful, Mallory. What in the hell am I going to do about you?"

Love me, her mind whispered. That was what he could do. Just give up the battle and love her as much as she loved him.

"Let's go," he said gruffly, then spun around and strode to the door.

The mountain home was just that, a home, and Mallory was delighted as Michael led her through the rooms. Hardwood floors gleamed, the massive dark furniture looked comfortable and inviting. There were two bedrooms, a modern kitchen done in blue and white, and a large stone fireplace in the living room. There was also, Michael pointed out with a great deal of fanfare, a fully equipped bathroom connecting the two bedrooms.

"Big deal," Mallory said, and sniffed indignantly. Michael hooted with laughter.

A roaring fire was soon going in the fireplace, and the furnace was clunking and groaning as it was pressed into action.

"This is a lovely home, Michael," Mallory said.

"Yeah, I like it. I don't get up here as much as I used to, though. I've gotten busier, and one week seems to slide into the next. Now that I'm here, I realize I've missed this place. It's so peaceful, soothing, a total escape from it all."

Not this time, Mallory thought with bitter irony as Michael headed outside to get their stuff. He'd brought his problem with him. Her.

Her glance fell on the open doors to the bedrooms. Each had a double bed and had been decorated with a masculine flair. Which was Michael's room? she wondered. He would, of course, put her suitcase in one, his in the other. Michael Patterson had no intention of making love with her. Oh, he wanted her, no doubt about it. Her self-esteem was doing fine as far as knowing that he desired her. But he wouldn't succumb to those desires. Not tough-guy Michael.

She stared into the leaping flames in the fireplace, then turned as she heard Michael reenter the house. He had his suitcase in his hand, her bag slung over his shoulder, and a box of food cradled in his other arm. He kicked the door closed behind him, set their bags on the floor against the wall, and carried the box into the kitchen.

Now, what did *that* mean? Mallory wondered, gazing at the suitcases. It meant nothing. Absolutely nothing. Michael had been juggling a cumbersome load, and had simply rid himself of part of his cargo. She wasn't going to start becoming paranoid about everything he did, for Pete's sake.

With a snort of self-disgust she went into the kitchen and offered to unpack the box of food.

"Sure," he said. "I'll go get the other one. Then do you want to go for a walk in the snow before lunch? I can put the screen in front of the fire, and off we'll go."

"Yes, that sounds like fun," she said, peering into the box. "Oh, marshmallows. I adore toasted marshmallows."

"It takes a pro to do them right. Burned on the outside, gooey on the inside."

"Absolutely," she said, laughing. "I wouldn't eat them any other way. See how much trouble we would have had arguing for our mothers' benefit, Michael? We even agree on how we like our toasted marshmallows."

"Yeah," he said quietly. "We do seem to have a great deal in common."

She quickly looked up at him, surprised at his sudden serious tone. She searched his face for some clue as to what had caused his mood switch. Before she could speak, though, he turned and left the room, mumbling under his breath about getting the other box of food.

Marshmallows made Michael moody? she wondered. It sounded like a tongue-twister rather than a reasonable explanation for his behavior. Was he disturbed because they shared the same interests? That didn't make sense. It had been quite a while since she'd colored him gray: confusing, unclear, foggy gray. But he was definitely acting gray.

When he returned to the kitchen in chipper spirits, exclaiming about the beauty of the freshly fallen snow, Mallory mentally threw up her hands in defeat and decided that psychoanalyzing people's words and actions was definitely not her forte.

After the food was put away, Michael set the screen in front of the fire, grabbed Mallory's hand, and hauled her out the front door.

"Look at this," he said, gesturing toward the snowy panarama with a wide sweep of his arm. "It's like a picture postcard."

Mallory tugged on her mittens. "Beautiful, but cold," she said. "We'd better keep moving before our blood freezes."

"It doesn't freeze *that* fast."

"Trust me. I know my blood. My toes are gone already. And my nose."

"No kidding?" He grinned at her. "What part of your anatomy is next?"

"Ears," she said. She hiked up her elbows and began to run in place. "Have to keep the circulation going."

Michael laughed as he took his gloves from his pocket and put them on. Mallory continued to jog, and from his other pocket he pulled a knitted blue hat.

"The ears I can fix," he said. "My mother made this for me."

"That's nice," she said, not stopping.

"Mallory, quit impersonating a pogo stick long enough for me to put this on you."

"Oh." She stopped. "But what about *your* ears?"

"My blood is macho. It won't freeze for at least twenty minutes."

He tugged the soft hat onto her head, checking to make sure her ears were completely covered. Then he slid his gloved hands slowly through her hair, drawing the long tresses forward to cover the front of her jacket. She stood completely still, hardly breathing as she gazed helplessly at his face, the face that was so close to hers. Their eyes met . . . and then their lips met.

Frozen toes, nose, and ears were forgotten as the heat of Michael's fiery kiss traveled through Mallory like an out-of-control forest fire. She ran her hands up his jacket to circle his neck as he gathered her close. Their heavy sweaters and coats did not diminish for Mallory the wondrous sensation of being held tightly in his arms, and she returned the kiss in total abandon. Giant, wet flakes of snow were covering them, but neither noticed. Finally Michael groaned deep in his chest and ended the kiss.

"I . . ." He began, then cleared his throat. He did not release his hold on her. "I don't know about you," he said, "but I've definitely warmed up. In fact, I overdid it a bit."

"Oh, Michael," she murmured. "Michael."

"Yes?"

"Nothing. Just, Michael. When you kiss me like that, I can't think of one intelligent thing to say."

"I can say that I want you, that I want to make love with you, but I'm not sure that's particularly intelligent."

"Why isn't it?" she asked, then took a deep

breath. Say it, she told herself. It was time to quit being coy, to quit playing games with cutesy innuendos. "I want to make 'love with you, Michael. I want you very much."

He drew in his breath sharply and his arms tightened around her. He stared up at the sky for a long moment, oblivious to the snow falling on him. When he looked at Mallory again, she was shocked to see a shadow of pain cross his face.

"I don't know what to do," he said, his voice strained. "I want you so damn much, Mallory. I've never been in a situation like this before. Never. I'm scared to death to take this step with you."

"Michael . . ."

"Come on," he said, releasing her and taking her hand. "Let's go for a walk. We have to remember your quick-freezing blood. How are the toes?"

"Fine," she said, smiling weakly.

She chewed nervously on the inside of her cheek as they walked down the driveway, then started along the narrow road. She glanced around at the tall trees that were rapidly becoming white statues of beauty, but the scenery had little effect on her. She was too aware of the strong hand holding hers, of Michael being next to her, and of the silence.

It was quiet, so very quiet, and she was sure Michael would hear the wild beating of her heart. And it was white, everywhere. What was the color white? she mused. Was it for things new? Beginnings? Or was this the elusive color of loneliness she had been searching for? Michael was struggling within himself, fighting so hard against his feelings for her. He wanted to make love with her, but he was so strong, could very well find the strength to turn away from her. Oh, Michael.

"Mallory," he said, breaking the stillness, "does my fear make sense to you? I know it's tacky to talk about the women in my past, but I want you to understand. I've never had sex just for the heck of it, just to satisfy the needs of my body. I gave as much as I took, I shared, I made love. The women were special in that I respected them, enjoyed their company out of bed as well as in. Lord, I can't believe I'm strolling along discussing my sex life."

"Go on," she said quietly. "I'm listening."

"I never made phony promises, I didn't lie. Those women knew where I stood. Yes, I respected and liked them, but I wasn't emotionally involved, not really. Does that sound lousy?"

"No, I understand."

"But it's different with you, don't you see? My emotions are totally out of whack about you. I had a knot in my stomach the size of a bowling ball when you were late getting home last night. I couldn't get Amy off·my mind because she was important to you, and . . . Hell, the list is endless. I'm feeling protective, possessive, even jealous. I haven't cared enough to be jealous since I was in the seventh grade. I'm telling you, Mallory, I'm really losing it here."

"And you're not happy about it, are you?" she asked, swallowing the lump in her throat.

"Hell, no, I'm not."

"People change, Michael."

"*I* don't. I told you that."

"Yes, I remember."

"And you agreed to help me through this. That's why we're here. I figure that by spending a great deal of time with you I'd . . . well, so far, all I've accomplished is to get an ache in my gut from wanting to make love with you. And with that thought comes the fear. I've never lov—been that emotionally involved when I made love with a woman."

"Just a good roll in the hay," Mallory said. Damn the man, she thought. She didn't know whether to burst into tears or hit him. He was taking on tinges of orange. Heaven forbid he should admit he cared for her. When he spoke of feeling protective of her, he made it sound as if he were diseased. Her nerves were already stretched to the limit. She couldn't take much more of this. "And a good time was had by all," she added, waving her hand breezily.

"Yeah, well, sort of. Not casual sex, you understand, but certainly not anything close to— Well, you know."

"Good Lord, Michael, is the word *love* so distasteful to you that you can't even say it? People fall in love every day. They get married, have babies, spend the rest of their lives together. It isn't a prison sentence; it's a way of living."

"Not for people like us, Mallory. We don't operate that way. We know exactly who we are, what we want, where we're going. No fuss, no muss, no clutter. We're two of a kind, like peas in a pod."

That tore it. A strange fury erupted in Mallory,

and she jerked her hand from Michael's. She was angry and hurt and confused, and didn't know where to put it all.

"How dare you tell me who I am and what I want," she said furiously.

"What? What's wrong with you?"

"You, that's what's wrong with me. You've stuck labels on me. You think you know me from A to Z, but you don't know me at all. I've done everything you've asked of me, followed your orders, mentally saluted. Well, guess what? I've had it! I have rights, too, Mr. Patterson. And I have dreams, and wants, and needs. You said making love is a mutually agreed upon decision."

He reached for her "Mallory—"

"Shut up," she said, backing away from him as her eyes misted with tears. "We haven't mutually agreed upon anything. You dictate. I do it. Well, no more. What about what I want? I want you to make love with me, Michael. I think it's crummy that you're so wrapped up in worrying about trying to separate your physical and emotional selves that you haven't given one thought to what all this is doing to me."

"Look, I—"

"Aren't I worth it, Michael?" she asked, moving farther back as tears spilled onto her cheeks. "Does everything have to be under your control? Isn't making love with me worth taking the risk of putting your emotions on the line?"

She took another step backward and thudded against the narrow trunk of a tree. The impact caused the branches to shake, bringing a heavy load of cold wet snow toppling down onto Michael.

"Aaagh!" he yelled. "Damn it, that's cold. It went inside my jacket!"

Why that was funny Mallory didn't know, but it was. So she laughed. She laughed until she was gasping for breath and holding her aching stomach. She laughed until her tears of pain and confusion were replaced by those of merriment. She laughed until she glanced at Michael's face. Then she stopped.

"Uh-oh," she muttered, seeing his thunderous expression.

"I'm glad you find this so humorous, Miss Carson," he said through clenched teeth as he advanced toward her.

Another bubble of laughter escaped from Mallory's lips, then she darted around Michael and took off running in the direction of the house. He spun around, lost his footing, and landed with a splat on his stomach in the snow.

"Come back here!" he roared.

He struggled to his feet, slipped once more, then started after her. She'd make better time if she quit laughing, Mallory thought gleefully as she sprinted toward the house. Those long legs of Michael's would cover the distance between them in a flash, and he was not exactly in a happy mood. He might murder her and toss her in a snow bank, and they wouldn't find her body until spring.

The house came into view, and she mentally cheered. She cut across the yard and tore in the front door. After slamming it shut, she leaned back against it with a sigh of relief. A moment later she was propelled forward as the door was flung open and Michael came barreling into the house. She skidded across the hardwood floor in her wet shoes until she connected with the back of the sofa. With less than graceful form she flipped over the top and landed in a heap on the soft cushions. In the next instant an enormous, wet person appeared around the end of the sofa and pounced on her, completely covering her body with his.

"Michael," she said, amusement still dancing in her blue eyes, "fancy meeting you here. You weigh a ton, by the way."

"No, *I* don't," he said. "That's snow. Heavy, wet, cold snow. Snow that has soaked me straight through to the skin. Snow that has frozen me into a solid block of ice. Snow dumped on me by you."

"I did not. The tree did it. Oh, you should have seen the look on your face. Priceless, absolutely priceless. Well, get off me so we can get into dry clothes."

"No."

"Pardon me?"

"No, I'm not getting off you."

"You're smushing me."

"I am not. My weight is on my arms and you know it."

"We'll catch pneumonia."

"The fire will warm us. You feel good beneath me, Mallory, bulky clothes and all. Very good."

"Oh," she said weakly, acutely aware of every masculine inch of him . . . bulky clothes and all.

"Every word you said is true," he went on. "I've been self-centered and selfish. I've been so blown away by my own inner turmoil that I didn't give a minute's thought to you, to your feelings. I'm sorry. I really am. I know you don't have casual sex with men, and I'm honored that you want to make love with me. And, Mallory, you're worth the risk of losing total control of my emotions. I'll deal with it on my own if it happens but, oh, yes, lady, you're worth the risk."

"Oh, Michael," she whispered.

"I'm going to make love *to* you and *with* you," he said, his voice husky with passion. "Right now. Right here on the rug in front of the fire. By mutual agreement. You do agree, don't you, Mallory?" he asked, his lips barely an inch from hers. "Don't you?"

Her "yes" was a breathy flutter of sound that was muffled by Michael's mouth claiming hers. The kiss was intoxicating, and she didn't even notice that he had unbuttoned her coat until she felt his gloved hand press flat on her stomach. The pressure sent shock waves of desire rocketing throughout her, and she shifted restlessly beneath him.

"Time out," he murmured, and pushed himself up off her. Standing next to the sofa, he quickly shed his gloves and jacket. Mallory struggled to sit up, then with slightly shaking hands removed her mittens, sodden shoes and socks, and the blue knit hat. She stood, her back to Michael, and slid her coat down her arms.

This was it, her heart sang. The moment she

had been waiting, praying for. She was about to make love with the man she loved.

"Mallory," he said.

The indigo-velvet sound of his voice, she thought dreamily, and turned slowly to face him.

Her pulse quickened as she gazed at him, drinking in the sight of his naked body. The firelight sent a glowing luminescence over him, transforming his tanned skin into bronzed beauty. Tawny curls covered the broad expanse of his chest and smattered along his muscled legs. His manhood boldly announced his desire for her.

This was Michael. Male. Magnificent. He was all, was even more, than she had ever imagined.

"Michael." His name was a plea on her lips.

He closed the distance between them and took her face between his hands. He kissed her forehead, her cheeks, the tip of her nose, her mouth. She ran her hands up his chest, relishing the feel of his soft hair and steely muscles. He grasped the bottom of her sweater and drew it up over her head. Then he removed her bra, and caught his breath at the sight of her loveliness.

"Beautiful," he said, filling his hands with her bare breasts. "You are so beautiful."

He placed his large hands on her waist and lowered his head to draw the rosy bud of one breast deep into his mouth. Mallory gasped with pleasure as she gripped his shoulders. He moved to the other breast and she arched her back, closing her eyes to savor each sensuous sensation. Michael flicked his tongue over the taut nipple of her sweetly aching breast as his hands unfastened her jeans.

Slowly, slowly, he drew the jeans down, his thumbs hooking into the waistband of her bikini panties as he went. His mouth followed, igniting her passion as he blazed a trail over her trembling body.

"Michael," she gasped. "Oh, please."

He knelt before her, paying homage to the silken skin of her thighs. Her legs refused to hold her any longer. She dropped to her knees before him and he sought her mouth with a vehemence that took her breath away.

In one powerful motion he lifted her, then fell back onto the thick rug, taking her with him. She was stretched out along his hard body as they continued to kiss ravenously. The only sounds in the room were the crackling fire and their harsh breathing.

Michael slid her higher up his body to gain access once again to her full breasts. He drew circles around them with his tongue, then took one into his mouth, suckling with a rhythm that matched the hot pulsing deep within her. She whispered his name, then moaned her pleasure.

He rolled over so that she was beneath him, catching his weight on his forearms. He looked directly into her eyes, and his own were dark with desire.

"Say it again," he said, his voice gritty with passion. "Tell me you want me. Tell me, Mallory."

"Yes, Oh, yes, I want you. Please, Michael, don't make me wait any longer. I need you so much."

He entered her slowly, watching her face as he filled her with himself. She smiled as she opened herself to him. He went deeper and deeper, and they were one. Then he kissed her, softly, reverently, and began to move.

He slid his arm beneath her hips to lift her to him as he began the ancient dance of love. She met each of his thrusts unhesitatingly, crying out with pleasure. The raging colors of passion flashed before her eyes as she clung to him, holding fast so as not to be hurled into oblivion.

Michael's loving was as she had known it would be: rich, honest. He was giving, and she gladly took all he offered, returning it to him with her heart. She soared higher and higher, seeking, striving, until the vibrant rainbow that surrounded her melted and became one with her in a burst of ecstasy.

"Michael!" she cried.

He fastened his mouth on hers as rapture swept through his body, toppling them both over the edge of reality. Then he collapsed against her, burying his face in the fragrant cloud of her hair. Neither moved nor spoke. The fire crackled as they lay quietly in its warming glow. Then he pushed himself up to gaze down at her flushed face.

"Incredible," he said, his voice unsteady. "I've never— Incredible."

"Yes, you are," she said, smiling.

"Not me. Us. Together. Am I crushing you?"

"No, you feel wonderful."

"I'll move away. Sometime next week." He trailed nibbling kisses down her throat.

"We might get hungry by then," she said, laughing softly.

He lifted his head to smile at her. "I'd even pass

up peanut butter and mayonnaise to make love with you."

"I'll be darned. No kidding?"

He nodded, then his smile faded. "I'm not going to think right now, Mallory," he said in a low voice. "What we just shared was fantastic. All I want to do is look at you, kiss you, feel you. I want to fill my senses with you, Mallory Carson. I'll think later," he said, lowering his head toward hers. "Much, much later."

Desire engulfed them once more. They flew together to the place of swirling colors and lingered there. Then Mallory drifted back slowly, holding Michael tightly to her. She pressed her lips to his shoulder, tasting the salty moistness of his skin.

He reached back and pulled an afghan off the sofa to cover them. There, in the soft glow of the fire, nestled in each other's arms, they slept.

Mallory opened her eyes and wondered vaguely where she was. As the fogginess of sleep dissipated she turned her head to gaze at a sleeping Michael.

So beautiful, she mused. Even in sleep, he had that aura of power, and was just so beautiful. Their lovemaking had been . . . There weren't words yet invented to describe it, to give meaning to such ecstasy. Dear heaven, how she loved him.

She moved just enough to get a glimpse of her watch, and was amazed to see it was after five o'clock. Her stomach growled as if to confirm the fact that the day had passed with no food since the early morning.

But she didn't want to leave the safe haven of

Michael's arms. She didn't want to wake him from his peaceful slumber, for then he would start to think about what had transpired between them. He said he would postpone any thinking, put the whole situation on one of his famous mental shelves, but it couldn't remain there forever.

What if he was angry with himself for succumbing to the physical needs of his body? What if he was sorry they had made love? No, Mallory decided, she wouldn't get gloomy, and look for trouble and heartache that hadn't materialized. But what if—

A warm hand slid across her bare stomach and she jerked in surprise.

"There's someone playing a bass guitar in there," Michael said, his voice husky with sleep. "Hungry?"

"Starving," she said, turning to smile at him.

"Let's shower, then eat. Separate showers, or we'll never eat. I'll be a gentleman and let you go first."

"You just want me to get the bathroom all warm and steamy for you."

"I'm going to get warm and steamy if you don't haul your cute tush out of here," he said, his hand inching toward her breast.

"Off I go."

She gave him a quick kiss, then dashed across the room. She grabbed her suitcase and in a few minutes was standing under the warm water in the shower. Her breasts were tender from Michael's lovemaking, her entire body stiff from her long nap on the floor. And she felt terrific. In Michael's bedroom she dressed in black brushed corduroy trousers and a mauve-colored angora sweater, then, humming softly, stepped into the living room.

Her smile faded rapidly as she looked at Michael. He had rebuilt the fire to a roaring blaze, and stood naked before it like a magnificent bronzed statue. His hands were gripping the mantel with such force that his knuckles were white. As she watched he drew a deep, shuddering breath, then his shoulders slumped as if the weight of his thoughts were crushing him.

A wave of icy fear washed over Mallory. A battle was raging inside Michael. Who would be the victor?

Eight

"The shower is all yours," Mallory said, forcing a tone of cheerfulness into her voice.

"What?" Michael turned to look at her. "Oh, yeah, I'll go right now." He dropped a quick kiss on her lips as he walked past her, then picked up his suitcase and disappeared into the bedroom.

Mallory watched him go, a heavy ache in her heart. He was, she decided, definitely doing the previously postponed thinking. The knot in the pit of her stomach told her she was not optimistic about the outcome.

With a sigh Mallory carried their damp clothes through the kitchen to the laundry room and hung them up. She then set the table and pulled the makings for a salad from the refrigerator.

"Steaks for dinner tonight," Michael said, striding into the kitchen. He was dressed in jeans and a burgundy-colored sweater. "Big, thick, juicy steaks. Good, you're making a salad. What else? I know. We'll warm that French bread. Man, I am starving."

She glanced up at him, searching his face for any clue that his lighthearted mood was forced, but saw none. He took two steaks from the refrigerator, exclaimed over their thickness, then rinsed them off and set them on the broiler in the oven.

She needed food, Mallory decided. Maybe after some nourishment, Michael's actions would make sense. She knew he'd been deep in thought by the fire. She'd practically felt the tension emanating from him. Now he was cheerful and happy. He was even whistling, for Pete's sake.

As she tore the lettuce she gazed out the window. The snow had stopped falling and night had come to the mountains. Heavy clouds were still hanging in the sky, obscuring the moon and stars. Mallory had the strange sensation that she and Michael had been lifted away and transported to another place, like Dorothy and the land of Oz. But that trip to the fairy-tale world had been a dream, and this was real. Dear heaven, she didn't want Michael to leave her. She loved him, wanted to spend the rest of her life with him. Talk about fairy tales.

"Hey, remember me?" he said, slipping his arms around her waist.

Jolted from her reverie, she glanced over her shoulder at him. "No. Who are you?"

"I'm the guy who made love with you in front of the fire."

"Did what? Where?"

He turned her around and pulled her up against

him. "Let's see if I can refresh your memory," he said.

His mouth melted over hers, and she sighed with pleasure. She splayed her hands over his back, savoring his honey-colored warmth. Her heart was racing when he lifted his head.

"Well?" he asked.

"I remember you," she said, smiling up at him. "Mikey, isn't it?"

He chuckled and swatted her bottom. As he turned the steaks over she slipped the bread into the oven to warm. Soon the aroma of bread and sizzling steak filled the air, and her stomach growled again,.

"I heard that," Michael said. "I'd better feed you before you faint dead away. Sit, madam; we are ready to dig in."

The food was delicious, and neither spoke for several minutes as they took the edge off their hunger. Mallory's fork was halfway to her mouth when she glanced up to see Michael staring at her, a frown on his face.

"Is something wrong?" she asked.

"No, I just . . . let's have this weekend, all right? No heavy talk, no soul searching. I want to be with you; laugh and talk; make love. Everything else can go on hold. I'm not telling you this is how it has to be, I'm asking. You were right when you said I'd been running the show. What do you think? Shall we forget about the rest of the world for now?"

"Yes," she said, smiling. "That sounds lovely." Borrowed time, she thought. Stolen moments. Foolish or not, she was going to do it.

"If you can't finish your steak," he said, leaning forward and peering at her plate, "I'll polish it off."

"You touch it and I'll stick you with this fork. I intend to eat every bite."

"Whew," he said, slouching back in his chair. "You're awesome in action."

"So are you, Patterson," she said, wiggling her eyebrows.

"I love it when you talk dirty," he said, chuckling.

She laughed. Throughout the remainder of the meal they chatted comfortably about movies they had seen, the current basketball season at the University of Arizona, and sundry other topics. They were still talking as they cleaned the kitchen together, Michael scrubbing the greasy broiler to within an inch of its life.

"Did Mary Louise teach you how to cook?" Mallory asked as she wiped off the table.

"Yep. She had me standing on a chair whipping up cakes when I was in kindergarten. Later, she taught me how to cook an entire meal. She said my wife would be my partner, not my maid. My father was in charge of laundry. He was very proud of the fact that he never turned anyone's underwear pink. My folks had enough money to hire a housekeeper to get it all done, but they felt it was important that I learn how to take care of myself."

"That's very nice," Mallory said. "It sounds as though you had a happy childhood."

"I did. Just about perfect. I got in a few fights at school, nothing major."

"Fistfights? Why?"

"Once our sixth-grade class had a bake sale and I told one girl her brownies were overcooked, and another that she should have double-sifted her flour for her cake because it was as heavy as a rock. The girl with the cake broke my nose."

"Serves you right," Mallory said, laughing.

"None of the boys hassled me about the cooking because I was bigger than they were. I went out for sports all through high school, and they learned real quick I'd have great stuff when we had to travel out of town on the bus. I like to cook. You start with nothing, and create whatever you want."

"You control the situation," she said quietly, pushing in the chairs at the table.

"Yeah, I suppose. I never thought of it like that before. Okay, we're done, spit-shined. Let's drink our coffee in front of the fire."

They sat on the rug and leaned back against the sofa, their legs stretched out in front of them. For a long time neither spoke.

"That fire is nearly hypnotizing," Michael said finally.

"Yes, I'm very mellow."

"Mallory . . ." He stared into his coffee mug. "I'm very glad you're here. This is nice, sitting in front of the fire with you. Thank you for— Well, everything."

Thank you, and good-bye? she wondered. It's been great, but see ya?

"Want to toast some marshmallows?" he asked.

"What? Oh, no, I'm still full from dinner. You go ahead if you want to."

"I'll wait." He stroked her hair back from her face. "I'd like you to sleep in my bed tonight, Mallory. I want to make love with you, then wake up next to you in the morning. Again I'm not dictating. I'm asking." He paused and looked directly at her. "Would you do that?"

"Yes. Yes, I will. How's this for worldly and so-phisticated? I've never spent the entire night with a man, never woken up with someone I—" Some-one I love, she finished silently. "What I mean is, I—"

He interrupted her. "I am delighted and honored to hear that. You're a rare and special woman, Mallory Carson."

She smiled at him warmly, and they gazed at each other for a long moment. An emotion Mallory couldn't decipher flickered across Michael's face, and she cocked her head slightly to study him.

"Do I have a bug on my nose?" he asked.

"No, you change moods very quickly sometimes, that's all. It's difficult to keep up with you. But then, I've known all along that you were a zoomer."

"Yeah," he said, turning to stare into the flames again. "A zoomer. An in-charge, in-control guy. Right?"

"Yes, I'd say that was an accurate description of you."

He laughed. A sharp, brittle laugh that sent a chill sweeping along Mallory's spine. She watched as he finished his coffee, then set their empty mugs on the hearth. After adding another log to the fire he settled back next to her with a weary-sounding sigh.

"What's wrong, Michael?" she asked. She placed her hand on his shoulder and felt the tension in his muscles. "I know you said you didn't want to have anything intrude on this weekend, but something obviously is. You're like a tightly coiled spring."

His head jerked around and he looked at her with a rather puzzled expression on his face.

"You know me that well?" he asked. "I always thought I did a good job of covering my feelings, hiding my problems. No one, except my mother, has ever seen beyond the picture I present."

"I know you that well," she said. "But, then, you sense when I'm upset too."

"You give more distinct clues. You dump a ton of snow on a person."

She laughed "I did not. It was the tree."

"I'll sue the tree. Ah, Mallory. Come here." He slid his arm around her shoulders. "No heavy thinking or talking, remember?"

She scooted closer, snuggling against him and resting her head on his shoulder. He stroked her arm in a lazy rhythm that sent shivers coursing through her.

"Cold?" he asked.

"Not at all."

The fire hissed and snapped as they stared into its flickering flames. Mallory smiled as she felt Michael relax, felt the tension ebb from his strong body.

Yes, she knew him, she thought. Knew him, and loved him. On the surface it seemed he knew exactly who he was and what he wanted. He was no doubt envied his ability to stay on his charted course by those who found themselves questioning and floundering.

But she knew better than that. Right now he was very uncertain, unnerved by the emotions she evoked in him. He was also fighting against them, angry that this should be happening to him.

He suddenly chuckled softly, and she tilted her head back to look at him.

"I was just thinking," he said, "about our mothers. If there really wasn't a bridge marathon, they might get bored and decide to try their hand at skiing."

"Oh, please, don't say such a thing. I shudder at the thought. I wouldn't put it past them though."

"They're something, aren't they?"

"Michael, how did your father die?"

"A small plane accident. A freak storm blew up over the mountains when he was flying home from Denver, and he crashed." His voice was flat, hiding the sorrow she was sure he still felt from the loss.

"I'm sorry, Michael," she said, touching his arm.

He sighed. "Yeah. How about your father?"

"Many years ago, the day before my mother's birthday, he had to go to Phoenix on business. He was determined to be with her on her special day, so he started driving back that night. He hadn't even left the city limits when he was hit by a drunk driver. The police called my mother, and she flew to the hospital in Phoenix. I was only ten, so she left me with a neighbor."

"And?"

"He lived for a few hours after she got there."

"Damn," Michael said, shaking his head. "Both our fathers were on their way home to their families when they died. And their wives were left alone." He pushed himself to his feet and stood in front of the fireplace, shoving his hands into the back pockets of his jeans as he stared into the flames.

"There are all kinds of risks in loving, Michael," Mallory said, "both physical risks and emotional ones. But I'm sure neither your parents nor mine would have done anything differently."

He didn't answer. He just continued to stare into the fire.

Oh, didn't he see? she thought. He'd taken a risk with his emotions when he'd made love with her. And now his fears were hovering just below the surface, showing themselves in fleeting glimpses of haunting pain on his face, in his eyes.

How she longed to go to him, to hold him in her arms and comfort and reassure him. She would declare her love again and again, tell him that the joys they could share would far outweigh the risks.

Those were only words, though. They could be crushed by the weight of his doubts and fears. What he felt for her was deep inside him, and had to be nurtured by her patience, her gentle touch. He cared for her, she knew he did. The tiny seed of love for her was nestled in his heart, waiting for the chance to grow. But left alone and neglected, it would die.

"Mallory," he said, his voice slightly strained as he turned to face her.

"Yes?"

"Would you like a toasted marshmallow?"

"I'd like about six toasted marshmallows," she said, smiling up at him.

"I'll get them," he said, and started toward the

kitchen. "I've got some long barbecue forks we can use."

She watched him stride from the room, understanding that he was pushing it all to the back of his mind again. So be it. She'd wait, and she wouldn't give him up without a fight. She had her pink satin ribbon of self-esteem. She had class. She had a heart overflowing with love for Michael Patterson.

He returned with the marshmallows and two long-handled forks, declaring he was the Marshmallow-Toasting Champion of the state of Arizona. She stuck her tongue out at him and announced she could beat him with her eyes closed.

"Your weapon, madam," he said, handing her a fork. "I just want to warn you that I plan to get serious about this. Burned on the outside, gooey on the inside, my marshmallows will be classified as culinary art."

"Sorry, chum," Mallory said. "You've met your match. I was the marshmallow champ of Girl Scout Troop Fourteen. You're messin' with a pro, Patterson."

"You don't stand a chance, Carson."

For the next hour they had a ridiculous and fun time. They ranted and raved, accused each other of cheating, whooped in delight when the opponent's marshmallow plopped into the fire, and ate their fill of the sweet snacks.

"I declare it a tie," Michael said finally. "I'm also dying. Why did I eat so many? My stomach is killing me."

"Really?" Mallory said. "I feel fine."

"Oh, yeah? You're always that shade of green, huh?"

She laughed and flopped back onto the rug, clutching her stomach.

"Just don't rock the boat," she said.

"What we need to do," he said, gently lowering his body over hers, "is think about something else to take our minds off the precarious state of our stomachs." He smiled down at her. "Any suggestions?"

"Well, let's see. We could talk about the weather, or the state of the economy."

"Two strikes," he said as his head slowly descended toward hers. "One more, and I'm up to bat."

"I have it. The zoning law regarding keeping horses within the city limits."

"You're out."

"Oh, good," she said, circling his neck with her arms. "Do I get sent to the showers now?"

"Later, after a long, long stopover in my bed."

"Don't you want your turn at bat first?"

"Wouldn't miss it for the world," he murmured, then claimed her mouth with his.

An urgency engulfed them instantly. Their passion raged as though a match had been set to dry grass. Mallory's heart thundered against her ribs as she met Michael's tongue with her own. She felt his arousal pressing against her, hard and full. A ragged moan echoed in her ears, and she didn't know if it had come from her throat or his, nor did she care. All she cared about was having Michael.

He rolled away from her and stood, then extended his hand to her. She placed hers in his, and allowed him to draw her up against him. Their lips met again in a searing kiss.

"I want you," he said huskily.

"Yes," was all she could manage to say.

He led her into the bedroom and turned on a small lamp on the nightstand. Then he drew Mallory into his arms and held her, simply held her, for a long heart-stopping moment. She rested her head on his chest and heard the wild beating of his heart. She slid her hands beneath his sweater, then inched her fingertips below the waistband of his jeans, feeling his muscles tighten at her feathery touch.

She moved back to tug his sweater up, standing on tiptoes to pull it over his head. As he reached for the buckle on his belt, she stilled his hands to perform the task herself. Then, as he had done for her in front of the fire, she eased the soft denim down his hips and legs. He stood naked before her as she knelt in front of him. He reached for her, but she shook her head.

"Let me love you," she whispered, trailing her fingers up the sides of his legs.

Her inflammatory kisses and sweet caresses caused him to clench his hands into tight fists. His breathing became ragged as her touch grew more intimate, and he trembled.

"I can't . . . take much . . . more of this," he rasped.

"You don't like it?" she asked, her voice unsteady.

"It's fantastic. You're fantastic. But . . ."

She stood and quickly shed her clothes, then pressed her nude body against his. They both gasped at the intoxicating feeling, and Mallory slid her hands seductively down his chest, then lower, and lower, and—

"Enough!" Michael said, grabbing her arms.

He swept her over to the bed and followed her down onto it. Without hesitation she opened herself to him, and he entered her with a thrust that stole her breath away. He drove deep, deep, so deep within her, until she thought she would shatter. Their loving was swift, hard, but no less caring. Together they strove for release, and when they found it, it exploded upon them with the wild fury of a tempestuous storm.

In the silence that followed they clung to each other, drifting back slowly to the real world.

"Oh, Michael," Mallory whispered.

"I know."

"Wonderful."

"Unbelievable. I should get off you."

"Don't go. Stay right where you are."

"You talked me into it. You feel so damn good."

"So do you."

"I was too rough with you, Mallory."

"No. No, it was fantastic."

"You drove me out of my mind. Where did you learn to— Forget it, I don't want to know."

"You taught me in front of the fire earlier. I've never done anything like that before. I wanted to give to you just as you had to me."

"You're a fast study."

"You enjoyed it?"

"I nearly died, but they would have found my corpse smiling from ear to ear. I now understand the term *heaven and hell*."

"And I understand making love. We do, you know. Make love."

"I told you we would, remember?"

"I remember."

"I really should get off you. I—Mallory, quit wiggling like that or you're going to start something I'll be only too happy to finish."

"Wiggling? Like this? Or like this? Which of these wigglings do you want me to quit doing?"

"Too late."

"Oh, thank goodness."

Much, much later they slept, heads resting on the same pillow, Mallory's tucked beneath Michael's chin. When she stirred, he automatically tightened his hold on her, though neither of them woke. A sudden wind whipped against the window as if seeking entry to the warm haven within, then skittered away as if knowing not to intrude upon the contented slumber of the couple in the quiet room.

The first of Mallory's senses to emerge from her cocoon of sleep was that of smell. Coffee. The rich aroma prompted her to open one eye to see a large, tanned hand wraped around a mug directly in front of her nose.

"Coffee," she mumbled, opening the other eye.

"Got it in one," Michael said. "I don't have to get hit with a brick twice, you know, to figure things out. My lady is not quite herself before her morning coffee. Madam, your coffee."

She slowly shifted her gaze upward, deciding in her foggy state to postpone the delicious moment when Michael would come into view. Her gaze traveled over a bare chest covered in tawny curls, wide shoulders, a strong neck, then his face. His beautiful, smiling face.

Memories of their lovemaking filtered through the haze, and she smiled, too, feeling the familiar stirrings of desire deep within her. She met Michael's gaze.

He drew in his breath sharply. "That is one very sultry, sexy look you're giving me there, kid."

"I'm just remembering"—she yawned—"some very sultry, sexy things we shared."

"For shame. What's a nice girl like you doing in a memory like that?"

"Enjoying every detail," she said, shifting the pillow behind her and sitting up.

He grabbed the sheet and covered her bare breasts. As he dropped his hand, the sheet slid back down to her waist.

He moaned. "Give me a break, Mallory."

"Hmm?" she said, all innocense.

"Here. Drink this. You're so weird before your caffeine fix, it's sad."

She laughed softly. He gave her a quick hard kiss, then strode from the room. She admired the view, since he was only wearing tight jeans that rode low on his hips. With a contented sigh, she sipped the steaming coffee.

"My lady," she repeated silently. That was what Michael had called her. His lady. It probably meant nothing significant to him, but it sounded wonderful to her. Michael's lady, his love, his woman, his wife, the mother of his— Halt! She was definitely getting carried away. She really shouldn't think before she'd had her coffee.

She glanced at the clock and frowned when she saw that it was after ten. The day was flying by, and soon they would drive down the winding mountain road and return to reality. And tomorrow Michael was leaving for California for three days. And nights.

"Ugh," she said. And what about when he returned from California? she wondered. Would he use the time away from her to sort through his jumbled thoughts about what had happened between them, and decide what he was going to do about her? There she was again, sounding like a pesty fly. She'd concentrate on sultry, sexy; on being Michael's lady. No gloom and doom today. Not today.

"Breakfast in ten minutes," Michael yelled.

"Coming," she called. She drained her mug, then threw back the blankets and headed for the shower. When she entered the kitchen several minutes later, Michael was setting plates of eggs, bacon, and toast on the table.

"Right on time," he said, turning to face her. He pulled her into his arms. "Drink the whole mug full? Are you human? You smell good and look fantastic. I'll check out how you taste and feel."

The kiss he gave her was long and sweet, and her legs were trembling when he released her.

"All systems are go," he said. "Good morning, Mallory Carson."

"Hello, Michael Patterson."

"Let's eat while it's hot. Then we'll build a snowman. A small snowman, due to the fact that most of the snow has melted. Sit."

As they ate, Mallory asked Michael about the conference he was attending. He told her it was being held at the Hilton Hotel in Los Angeles, and that attorneys from all across the country would be there. Yes, indeed, he was the keynote speaker, he went on, and if she treated him right, he'd give her his autograph. She plopped a blob of strawberry jelly on top of his eggs. He thanked her politely and ate every bite.

The air was clear, crisp, and cold. Mallory did her running-in place routine until Michael rolled his eyes and hauled her toward the patches of snow still remaining beneath the trees. The snowman was all of two feet high, and faded fast as the sun was creeping higher in the sky. When its head slid off and landed with a wet splat on Mallory's foot, she wailed in dismay. They settled for a snowball fight, both declaring themselves the winner, then finally returned to the house soaked to the skin.

"Hot shower," Michael said, his teeth chattering.

"Me, too. Me first," Mallory said, peeling off her wet jacket. "Oh-h-h, I'm cold. My blood is frozen, I'm sure of it. Bye."

She ran into the bathroom and had no sooner stepped into the hot shower, when a naked Michael joined her. She gasped in surprise, then smiled.

"Scrub your back, ma'am?" he asked.

"Okay. Then I'll scrub your front."

"Uh-oh," he said, chuckling. "I think I'm in trouble."

"Heaven and hell, Michael. Heaven and hell."

"I'm tough. I can handle it. I—Mallory!"

Drying each other with fluffy towels was their final undoing. They tumbled onto the bed and came together with a feverish urgency. They soared, they lingered, they drifted slowly back.

As they lay in each other's arms, Mallory drew tiny circles on Michael's chest with her fingertip as he lazily stroked her back.

"Well," he said finally, "I suppose we'd better get this show on the road. We have to close up the house, then repack the food we didn't use."

"And pick up the mothers."

"Yeah. I do not, absolutely do not, want to think about what they've gotten themselves mixed up in."

"Maybe they really did play bridge."

"Don't bet on it."

"They're going to be watching us like hawks, looking for some clue as to how we got along."

"Cool and loose, sweetheart," he said.

She laughed. "Oh, good Lord."

It took well over an hour for them to pack and close up the house. The last of the supplies were finally loaded into the Bronco, and Michael locked the front door.

"I hate to leave," Mallory said. "It was wonderful—all of it, every minute."

"Indeed, it was," Michael said, kissing her quickly. "Ready?"

"Yes," she said. No, she thought. She wanted to hear him say that they would come back again. What had this weekend meant to Michael? Did he see her as a part of his future, as his lady? Or had he accomplished his damnable cure, and would he now say good-bye? She loved him so much, and the polite thing for him to do would be to love her back. Lord, she was getting hysterical.

When they stopped at the lodge, Michael loaded Clarissa's and Mary Louise's luggage as the two women climbed into the backseat.

"Hello, dear," Clarissa said to Mallory.

"Hi," Mallory said as Michael got back in the Bronco. "How was the bridge marathon?"

"Exhausting," Mary Louise said. "I'm going to sleep for a week. Starting now." She leaned her head back and closed her eyes.

"Wake me when I'm home," Clarissa said, also closing her eyes.

Mallory and Michael exchanged shrugs, then he drove back to the road and started down the mountain.

With every passing mile the knot in Mallory's stomach tightened. She glanced often at Michael, but there was no clue as to what he was thinking. The trip was made in total, oppressive silence.

Nine

Mallory felt as if there were a movie playing in her head on Monday. No one at the Honey Bee asked her if she had lost her mind, so she assumed she appeared to be functioning normally. Still, the events of the weekend replayed in her mind over and over, often bringing a warm flush to her cheeks as desire tingled throughout her. Then there was the last scene, the one that had taken place in her apartment.

Clarissa and Mary Louise had been deposited at their respective homes, and Michael had driven Mallory to her apartment. In her living room he had declined her offer of food and drink, and had even refused to take off his jacket. He had to go home and pack for his trip, he had said. It sounded reasonable, but Mallory had sensed how on edge he was again. His tension, and his quick good-bye kiss and mumbled farewell, hadn't helped her already jangled nerves.

Monday dragged by in a series of seemingly endless hours. The only bright spot was when Amy's mother told Mallory Amy had spent a happy weekend with her father. But then Patty commented on how wonderful that Mikey Patterson was, and the movie started once again in Mallory's mind.

The fact that it was raining when she left the Honey Bee seemed appropriate, as did her lack of an umbrella. Cold and wet, she let herself into her apartment and headed for a hot shower. Clad in a terry-cloth robe that had seen better days and her favorite scruffy slippers, she then ate a dinner consisting of canned spaghetti and an orange.

After recalling, for perhaps the hundredth time, making love with Michael in front of the fire, she decided enough was enough. To relive precious memories was all very well and good, but it was not facing the problem at hand. Said problem being, she had no idea if she'd ever see Michael Patterson again. Lord, what a horribly depressing thought.

When the telephone rang, she hurried to answer it, hoping it was Michael.

"Hello?"

"Hello, dear," her mother said.

Darn it, Mallory thought. "Hi, Mother. Did you recover from your wild weekend?"

"Yes, I'm all rested. Mallory, I want to talk to you about Michael."

"What about him?" she asked, sinking onto the sofa, her heart racing.

"I'm concerned about your relationship with him."

"Concerned? I thought you were thrilled."

"Well, I was until I had a lengthy discussion with Mary Louise while we were at the lodge. Michael is dead set against marriage, Mallory. He has no intention of ever settling down with one woman."

"I know," she said quietly. "He has very strong views on the subject."

"Which are the complete opposite from yours, dear, unless you've changed your mind about getting married."

"No, I haven't."

"It worries me that you and Michael are so far apart on what you want. You're going to be terribly hurt if you fall in love with him. I realize I'm meddling, but I had to speak my piece. Be careful, dear, please. I don't want to see your heart broken."

"Thank you for your concern, Mother. I love you, you know. Don't worry about a thing. I'm very aware of Michael's stand on commitment. And since I am aware of it, I can't possibly be hurt, right? Right."

"Oh, that does relieve my mind. Well, I must go. Mary Louise and I are going to a club to see male strippers."

"What? That's absurd. Why?"

"Why are we going? Because we've never been before, of course. Life is just one nonstop adventure. And it's not absurd. It will, hopefully, be as sexy as all get out."

"Mother!"

"Ta-ta, dear."

"Ta-ta," Mallory said, shaking her head as she replaced the receiver. Her *mother* was going to see male strippers? What would that woman do next?

At least she'd convinced her that all was well. Mallory knew Michael was a confirmed bachelor, so there was no problem. No problem? Hah!

The phone rang twice more that evening. Both times it was a man Mallory had dated a few times, asking if she were free that weekend. She said no, that she had plans, even though Michael had said nothing about their getting together when he came back from California. Was he forcing a distance between them already? she wondered. Was he that afraid of intimacy?

Or. . . . She sat up straight on the sofa, stunned by the thought that had just occurred to her. Michael thought *she* was avoiding commitment, too, that she had her life exactly the way she wanted it. Why would he try to get rid of someone whose values he assumed were the same as his? Because he loved her.

He did love her, she was sure of it, and he was probably scared to death. She had to show him that she loved him, but that she would accept whatever commitment he was able to make, that she wouldn't ask for more than he was willing to give.

Feeling confident that everything would finally work out, she went to bed that night with a smile on her face.

Mallory was delighted with her optimistic mood the next day. The thought of Michael brought a smile to her lips and a warm glow to her heart. She was prepared to make major concessions in her life, but her pink satin ribbon of self-esteem was firmly in place. She would happily give up some of her dreams for the love of Michael Patterson.

At ten o'clock that night he called.

"Hi!" she exclaimed when she heard his voice. "How's Los Angeles?"

"Smoggy. Look, I've got to make this quick. I'm meeting some people for a late dinner. I'm taking an earlier flight tomorrow. Could you meet me at my house at, say, seven tomorrow night? There's a key under the front mat."

"Well, yes, all right, but why?"

"We have to talk. I'm getting away from here as quickly as I can. Do you have a pencil and paper? I'll give you directions to my place."

"Yes, go ahead," she said. As she scribbled down the directions she was aware that her hand was trembling. "I've got it."

"Seven o'clock then. If I'm later than that, wait for me. Okay?"

"Yes, of course. But—"

"Good. I'll see you at the house. Mallory . . ."

"Yes?"

"Nothing. Bye."

"Good night, Michael," she said softly, then slowly replaced the receiver.

Mallory sank onto the edge of the sofa and pressed trembling fingers to her lips. She didn't want to talk to Michael! she thought frantically. She wanted to see him, kiss him, make love with him, but she did *not* want to hear what he had to say. He'd sounded so tense on the phone. Why was he insisting they meet at his house, rather than here at her apartment? And, oh, dear heaven, what was he going to say to her? Was this it, the end of it all?

"Oh, Michael," she whispered in the quiet room, "aren't we going to have our chance to run the risks, and love each other?"

The night was long and lonely. Mallory tossed and turned, trying desperately to sleep. She kept having the ridiculous thought that if she didn't go to Michael's house, he couldn't tell her what she didn't want to hear, and it would, therefore, not be true. At last she dozed, only to be plagued by haunting dreams of Michael Patterson.

By noon the next day Mallory couldn't take the noise and confusion at the Honey Bee. She pleaded a headache, which was actually the truth, and left Patty in charge of the boisterous children. Mallory wandered aimlessly through a shopping mall, ate a lunch she didn't taste, and bought two silk shirts and a skirt that she didn't really want. But anything was better than sitting alone in her apartment.

At six-thirty she drove to Michael's.

The ranch house was located in the affluent foothills area, and she got lost twice trying to find it. The key was under the mat, as Michael had said it would be, and she had the vague thought that that was not a brilliant place to leave a spare key.

Once inside she stepped into the living room. There was a light switch on the wall, and she flicked it. Immediately four lamps came to life.

"Oh," she gasped, staring wide-eyed.

The room was large and beautifully decorated in warm colors and comfortable-looking furniture. The chocolate-brown carpeting was plush beneath her feet, and the floor-to-ceiling bookshelves on

one wall beckoned to her explore their treasures. But she just sat motionless in an over-
stuffed armchair, her heart pounding painfully, as
she waited for Michael. When the telephone rang
shrilly, she jumped in fright.

"Now what?" she muttered. Should she answer
it? No, of course not. This wasn't her house, that
wasn't her phone. But what if it was Michael
making sure she'd gotten there? Maybe he'd been
delayed. Oh, the heck with it. She snatched up the
receiver. "Hello?"

"Yeah. Is Mike there?" a deep, gruff voice asked.

"Mike? You mean Michael? Michael Patterson?"

"Yeah. Is he there?"

Something in the man's voice disturbed Mallory,
but she simply said, "No, but I expect him any
minute. May I take a message?"

There was a long silence, and she could hear
the man's harsh breathing. This wasn't right, she
thought. Who was this man?

"If you'd give me your name . . ." she began
tentatively.

"Where the hell is he?" the man suddenly exploded. "I've got to talk to him!"

"Oh, Lord," Mallory breathed, willing her heart
to slow. "He should be here any minute," she said
as calmly as she could, even as she wondered if
she should just hang up. But this man must
know Michael. Maybe he was one of Michael's
clients. Yes, that was why he sounded so frantic.
He was upset and wanted to talk to his lawyer.

"Sir—" she started, but he interrupted her.

"I've got to talk to him," the man said, and the
anguish in his voice was even more frightening.

"Where is he? I've already called his office."

"He's been— Oh, wait. I think I hear him." She dropped the receiver onto the table and ran to the window in time to see Michael wearily climb out of his car. She hurried to the front door and met him there.

"Hello, Mallory," he said quietly, dropping his garment bag on the floor.

"Michael, there's a man on the phone who wants to talk to you. He sounds . . . he sounds awful."

Michael frowned, and pushed past her into the living room. "This is Michael Patterson," he said into the receiver.

Mallory studied him as he listened to the man on the other end. He looked beautiful, but exhausted. Now his brows were drawing together in consternation, and his whole body suddenly stiffened.

"No!" he said into the phone. "Don't do anything. Don't hurt her. I'll be right over." He paused to listen, then said, "I've got the address. I'll be there in twenty minutes. Don't do anything!"

He hung up the phone and turned toward her. "Mallory . . ."

"Michael, what is it? Who was that man?"

"He's a client of mine, Tom Brewster. He—he hasn't been coping well with his divorce. Oh, God." He rubbed his hands over his face. "I've got to get over there," he said. "He's got his ex-wife held up in her house, and he has a gun."

Mallory froze in horror. A gun? And Michael was going over there? "Michael! You can't go. He—he might kill you."

"Mallory, I have to go. He's my client . . . but it's

more than that." He paused, then said softly, "I have to go."

Time seemed to stop for Mallory. Risks, she thought. None were too great when dealing with love. A man had to be true to his convictions, and the woman who loved him had to understand that.

"Yes, Michael," she said quietly, realizing this was something he had to do. This was the kind of man he was. "You have to go. I understand."

He stared at her, puzzled.

"I'll go back to my place," she continued, "and wait for you there."

"Mallory . . ." He took a step toward her. "Mallory, thank you. I'll come to you as soon as I can." Then he turned and sprinted out the front door.

"I love you," she said to the empty room. "I love you, Michael."

The telephone rang, and Mallory nearly fell off the sofa. She looked around, trying to figure out where she was. As she groped for the phone she realized she must have fallen asleep waiting for Michael to call. What time was it now? she wondered.

"Hello?" she said groggily into the phone.

"Mallory? It's Patty."

"Patty? What time is it?"

"About six."

"In the morning? Yes, of course, in the morning," Mallory said, struggling to sit up. "Is something wrong?"

"Andy has a slight fever and a sore throat. I'll

have to stay home with him today. Are you all right? You left early yesterday with that headache."

"I'm fine. I'll go to the Honey Bee, and you take care of Andy."

"I'm sorry about this, Mallory."

"Don't be. Give Andy a hug for me."

"I will, and thanks. Hopefully, he'll be okay by tomorrow. I'll check in with you later."

"Fine. Bye."

"Bye, boss. You're a gem."

Mallory stared at the telephone after hanging up. Where was Michael? Why hadn't he called or come over? What had happened with that man, Brewster? She didn't want to go to the Honey Bee. She'd told Michael she'd be here at her apartment, waiting for him. But she had to go to work if Patty wasn't going to be there. All she could do was leave a note on the door telling Michael where she'd gone. Darn it, where was he? Brewster had had a gun and— No, no gruesome thoughts.

The telephone rang again.

"Oh, Lord," she gasped, then picked up the receiver. "Yes?"

"It's Michael."

"Thank goodness," she said, squeezing her eyes closed. "Are you all right?"

"Yeah, just out on my feet."

"What . . . what happened? Did you convince Brewster not to hurt anyone, Michael?"

He sighed wearily. "No one was hurt. I talked to Brewster for hours and finally calmed him down. He's in police custody now.

"Mallory, I'm so tired right now I don't know my own name. I wouldn't make any sense if I tried to talk to you this morning. Are you going to the Honey Bee?"

"I have, to. Patty is staying home because her son isn't feeling well."

"Okay. Look, I'll get some sleep, and come over to your place tonight."

"Yes, fine," she said, the knot tightening in her stomach again.

"We have to talk. It's important."

"I know," she said quietly. "I'll see you tonight. Get some sleep, Michael. You sound exhausted."

"I am. See ya."

"Good-bye," she said to the dial tone.

It had been, Mallory decided as she walked down the hall to her apartment, the longest day of her entire life. The clocks had seemed to refuse to move forward, and bring her closer to seeing Michael. But when she thought of seeing him, she became afraid again of what he would say, and would want to postpone their meeting. She was a jumble of contradiction, had a roaring headache, and felt about ninety-two years old.

With a weary sigh she inserted her key in the door and stepped into her apartment. She closed the door behind her, then turned and stood perfectly still.

Every spare inch of her living room was covered in . . . stuff.

There was a five-foot tall bright pink plastic flamingo standing on one leg, a bird cage with no door, a multitude of figurines, candy dishes, and pieces of pottery. A bronze Buddha with a clock in his belly grinned at her, and a family of ceramic ducks were in a row on the carpet.

Her horrified gaze swept over a heart-shaped red satin fringed pillow with the name ZELDA stitched across it, then on to three baseball caps and six of the ugliest vases she had ever seen. A *Venus de Milo* was minus her head as well as her arms, and an Indian headdress done in brightly colored feathers leaned against the bookcase.

She'd been robbed, she thought. A burglar had— No, no. Burglars took things out, they didn't bring them in. She was in the wrong apartment. Oh, please, someone tell her she was in the wrong apartment. No, her key had worked in the door. She lived here. So, this was what a nervous breakdown felt like. When you went, you went big, right over the edge.

"Hello, Mallory," a deep voice said.

"Hi, Michael," she said, waving breezily as he came out of the kitchen. A slightly hysterical giggle escaped from her lips. "That's good," she continued, nodding. "Now I'm imagining that Michael is here too. Fascinating. Complete mental collapse is extremely fascinating."

"Mallory, I'm really here, and so is everything you're seeing in this room."

She sniffed indignantly. "Don't be absurd."

"I borrowed Clarissa's key," Michael said. He made his way to her, stepping over the duck family, a tarnished spittoon, and a stack of dog-eared *National Geographics*.

She poked him in the chest with a finger. "You're real," she said. "I'll be darned."

"Have we established the fact that you haven't flipped your cork?"

"What in the name of heaven have you done to my apartment?" she shrieked.

"Good. You're back to normal. I realize this a bit of a shock but—"

"Shock! It's a disaster. I've never seen so much junk in one spot before. I thought you said we were going to talk, not have a yard sale!"

"Come sit down."

"Where?"

"I'll move the snow shoes and the fishing poles off the sofa. Come on."

"Why not?" Mallory said, throwing up her hands.

Michael cleared off the sofa then sat down, patting the cushion next to him. She sank onto it, and they faced each other. He studied her for a long moment, then raked his fingers through his hair.

"I want to kiss you so damn much," he said, "but we've got to talk."

"About the yard sale?"

"About us! Mallory, I brought this stuff here to hopefully prove a point. I've gone through everything a thousand times in my mind, trying to figure out what to do. You knocked me over the minute I met you, you know that."

"And you hated it."

"Yeah, I did. My life was on course, exactly the way I wanted it, just like yours is."

"But you misunderstood how I— Never mind. Go on."

"I really thought that if I spent a great deal of time with you in a pseudocommitment-type set-up, I'd get back on track, reaffirm that I wanted no part of a permanent, or even long-term, relationship. You agreed to the plan, and we were off and running. The thing is, Mallory, it didn't work."

"What do you mean?"

"After we made love that first time and you had gone to take your shower, I had the weirdest feeling. You'd only left the room, were no more than a few yards away, but I suddenly had an image of what it would be like if you didn't come back. I've never felt so empty, so lonely. At that moment, Mallory, I realized, I knew, that I . . . that I loved you."

"Oh, Michael," she said, tears springing to her eyes.

"I didn't know what to do. I knew you had your life arranged the way you wanted it, and it sure as hell didn't include a husband and children. That's how far, how fast, my mind went. I wanted it all, with you. While I was in L.A. I thought it through again and again. Mallory, I believe that you care for me."

"Yes. Yes, of course I do."

"You wouldn't have made love with me if you didn't. I was hanging onto that thought for dear life. Then last night, at my house, I saw something more. I'd asked you to meet me there so you could see my home, discover another part of me, but then all hell broke loose with Brewster. I knew you were frightened because I was walking into a potentially dangerous situation, then suddenly you just seemed so calm, so accepting. You were willing to take the risk. I'm praying I'm not wrong about that. I'm hoping, praying, that you are in love with me."

"Oh, Michael," she murmured, tears spilling onto her cheeks.

"Do you?" he asked. His voice broke slightly. "Do you love me?"

She flung herself against him, wrapping her arms around him and burying her face in his neck. His own arms came around her and held her tightly.

"Yes, I love you," she said. "I love you so much, Michael."

"Thank God." His hold tightened even more. "We'll compromise. I know I can't have it all my way. I want to marry you, but we'll just live together if you'd rather. Just be with me, Mallory," he said, his voice oddly husky. "I need you, I love you. I want to spend the rest of my life with you."

She lifted her head to look at him. "Listen to me. Right after I met you I became somewhat confused about who I was and what I wanted."

"You said you were a befuddled mess."

"Yes, I was, but not for long. But somehow in the midst of it all, you assumed some things about me that weren't true. Michael, I very much want to get married, to have children. But I fell in love with you, and you said you wanted none of those things. I kept hoping you'd come to love me and maybe change your mind."

"Are you saying that you'll marry me?" he asked, gripping her shoulders.

"Yes, yes, yes," she said, smiling through her tears.

"I love you, Mallory," he said, then he kissed her.

The kiss spoke of love, of greater understanding, the end of doubts, the promise of beginnings. Mallory felt herself melt against him as her passion rose.

Finally he pulled away. "I want to make love with you," he murmured.

"Yes, I want you too. I— wait a minute!" She pushed against his chest. "What about all this junk in here? You said it was to prove a point. I've obviously missed that point."

"Oh, well, I went out to the swap meet with the idea of picking up a couple of knickknacks to put in here. It was going to represent a bit, just a bit, you understand, of clutter in your uncluttered living room. Then I was going to plead my case, and say that loving me wouldn't totally disturb your uncluttered life any more than a few doo-dads had wreaked havoc with your apartment. Clever, huh?"

"This, Mr. Patterson," she said, with a sweep of her arm, "is not 'a few doodads.' "

"But, Mallory, I couldn't pass this stuff up. It's really great. There are things here for every room in the house, every activity. I'm telling you, I got some terrific bargains. Hey, somewhere in here is a nose mitten. I got that for you for when we go to the Lemon. Oh, and there's a—"

"Michael," she interrupted, placing her hands on his cheeks and smiling warmly, "I love your doodads, and I love you. Make love with me, Michael. Now. Please."

With a throaty groan he lifted her into his arms and made his way carefully across the room, step-ping over and around the assembled treasures.

Their lovemaking was slow, sweet, sensuous. Roaming hands, lips, and tongues trailed heated paths over glistening bodies. It was the color of fire, of earth; it was ebony and dusky blue. They were one, a kaleidoscope of vibrant colors melting into one another.

Afterward they lay together, gently holding on to each other.

"I love you, Mallory," Michael said.

"And I love you. I must be out of my mind, though. I've just agreed to become one of the M and M's."

He chuckled as he sifted his fingers through the silken cascade of her hair. "Our mothers will be so damn smug, you know. I'm sure they'll figure out a way to claim they were responsible for us getting together."

"That's all right," Mallory said.

"Tomorrow we shop for wedding rings."

She stifled a yawn. "Okay."

"And," he went on, "I really think you should pay me what you owe me."

"What?" she said, very much awake again.

"People should go into marriage with a clean slate. No secrets between them, and definitely no debts. Yep, you should pay up, Mallory Carson."

"I don't know what you're talking about, Michael Patterson."

He grinned. "You owe me a piece of pecan pie!"

She laughed and kissed him soundly on the mouth. "I'll bake you a hundred," she said. "Oh, Michael, we have so much together, so very much. For the rest of my life, just color me happy!"

THE EDITOR'S CORNER

We have Valentine's Day presents galore for you next month . . . hearts, flowers, chuckles, and a sentimental tear or two. We haven't wrapped your presents in the traditional colors of the special holiday for lovers, though. Rather, we're presenting them in a spectrum of wonderful earth colors from vibrant, exhilarating Green to sinfully rich chocolate Brown. (Apologies to Billie and Sandra for using their last names this way, but I couldn't resist!)

First, in **MAKIN' WHOOPEE**, LOVESWEPT #182, by—of course—Billie Green, you'll discover the perfect Valentine's Day heroine, Sara Love. Ms. Love's business partner (and sweet nemesis) is the wickedly good-looking Charlie Sanderson. These two charmers have been waging a long silent battle to repress their true feelings for one another. He has built for himself a reputation as "Good Time Charlie," the swinging bachelor; she has built walls around her emotions, pouring all her energies into the business. An ill-fated trip to inspect a piece of property is the catalyst for the erosion of their defenses, but it isn't until a little bundle of joy makes an astonishing appearance that these two humorous and heartwarming and sexy people come together at last . . . and forever. With all the freshness, optimism, and excitement we associate with the green of springtime, Billie creates in **MAKIN' WHOOPEE** two characters whose love story you'll long remember.

TANGLES, LOVESWEPT #183, by Barbara Boswell, is a story that dazzled me so much I see it as painted in brilliant yellows and golds. Barbara's heroine, Krista Conway, is a highpowered divorce lawyer who is as beautiful as she is brainy. And to hero Logan Moore, the new judge who is trying Krista's case, she is the most seductive lady he's ever laid eyes on. Now Krista may appear hard as nails, but beneath her beautiful and sophisticated exterior is a

(continued)

tender woman who yearns for a man to love and a family to care for. Logan is one heck of a sexy widower with three delightful children . . . and he's a man who is badly misled by Krista's image and wildly confused by his compelling need for her. In a series of events that by turns sizzle with love and romance and sear with emotional intensity, the **TANGLES** these two wonderful people find themselves in begin to unravel to an unexpectedly beautiful ending. Bravo, Barbara Boswell!

The warm earth colors of orange, pale to dusky, had to have been on the palette of Anne and Ed Kolaczyk as they created **SULTRY NIGHTS,** LOVESWEPT #184. In this poignant romance of love lost and love regained, we encounter Rachel Anders years after her passionate affair with Ben Healey. One brilliant, erotic, tenderly emotional summer was all Rachel and Ben had together before he had to leave town. Rachel lived on in pained loss, faced with Ben's silence, and comforted only by the legacy of their passion, a beloved daughter. When they meet again, the attraction between them is fired to even greater heat than they'd known in their youth. But Rachel's secret still will come between them until they find their own path to a love that time could not destroy. Ablaze with intensity, **SULTRY NIGHTS** is a captivating love story.

Sandra Brown is a remarkably talented and hard-working author who seems phenomenal to me in the way she keeps topping herself in the creation of one wonderful love story after another. And here comes another of her delectably sensual love stories, **SUNNY CHANDLER'S RETURN,** LOVESWEPT #185. I referred above to "sinfully rich chocolate." I must have written those words because unconsciously I was still under the sway of a very short, but never-to-be forgotten episode in this book involving triple dipped strawberries. (See if you don't delight in that scene as much as I did.) And speaking of people who are

(continued)

phenomenal in topping themselves, I must mention Barbara Alpert who writes all the splendid back cover copy for our LOVESWEPTs. Her description of Sandra's next book is so terrific that I'm going to give you a sneak preview of the back cover copy. Here's what Barbara wrote.

"The whispers began when she entered the ballroom—and every male eye in the place was caught by the breathtakingly lovely spitfire with the slightly shady reputation. Ty Beaumont knew a heartbreaker when he saw one—and also knew that nothing and nobody could keep him from making her his inside a week's time. He'd bet a case of Wild Turkey on it! Sunny heard his devil's voice drawl in her ear, and couldn't help but notice the man was far too handsome for his own good, but his fierce ardor sparked hers, and his "I'll have you naked yet" smile caused a kind of spontaneous combustion that nothing could quench. Private torments had sent both Ty and Sunny racing from the past, but would revealing their dark secrets let them face the future together?"

We think next month offers you a particularly exciting quartet of LOVESWEPTs, and we hope you enjoy each one immensely.

With every good wish,

Carolyn Nichols

Carolyn Nichols
  Editor
LOVESWEPT
Bantam Books, Inc.
666 Fifth Avenue
New York, NY 10103